"Do You Always Get Your Way?"

Emily asked.

"You'd better believe it," Jeremy said with a grin, watching her face for a reaction.

"It's scary to think about."

"What is?"

"Marrying you—becoming a part of your life."

"Oh, that. To me the scariest thing would be not to marry you and not to have you as a part of my life." They lay there together for several moments without speaking. Finally Jeremy said, "Besides—"

When he didn't continue, she asked, "Besides what?"

"You lured me on with your delectable beauty, your intelligence, your luscious body. You seduced me, Emily. It's only fair that you do the honorable thing and marry me."

Dear Reader:

Welcome! You hold in your hand a Silhouette Desire—your ticket to a whole new world of reading pleasure.

A Silhouette Desire is a sensuous, contemporary romance about passions, problems and the ultimate power of love. It is about today's woman—intelligent, successful, giving—but it is also the story of a romance between two people who are strong enough to follow their own individual paths, yet strong enough to compromise, as well.

These books are written by, for and about every woman that you are—wife, mother, sister, lover, daughter, career woman. A Silhouette Desire heroine must face the same challenges, achieve the same successes, in her story as you do in your own life.

The Silhouette reader is not afraid to enjoy herself. She knows when to take things seriously and when to indulge in a fantasy world. With six books a month, Silhouette Desire strives to meet her many moods, but each book is always a compelling love story.

Make a commitment to romance—go wild with Silhouette Desire!

Best,

Isabel Swift
Senior Editor & Editorial Coordinator

ANNETTE BROADRICK
With All My Heart

Silhouette Desire

Published by Silhouette Books New York

America's Publisher of Contemporary Romance

SILHOUETTE BOOKS
300 East 42nd St., New York, N.Y. 10017

ISBN: 0-373-05433-5

First Silhouette Books printing July 1988

ANNETTE BROADRICK

lives on the shores of the Lake of the Ozarks in Missouri where she spends her time doing what she loves most—reading and writing romantic fiction. "For twenty-five years I lived in various large cities, working as a legal secretary, a very high-stress occupation. I never thought I was capable of making a career change at this point in my life, but thanks to Silhouette I am now able to write full-time in the peaceful surroundings that have turned my life into a dream come true."

To my friend Storm—

**Whose marvelous sense of humor
brightens even the darkest days**

One

Ms. Hartman?" A breezy male voice inquired when Emily answered the ringing telephone.

"Yes?"

"Is this Emily Hartman of 1402 Locust Street, Little Rock, Arkansas?" The unknown voice held an exuberance that sounded unusual, particularly when asking for Emily.

She glanced at her sister, Terri, who had come over from next door as soon as Emily had arrived home from work. They had been sitting at the kitchen table visiting over fresh cups of coffee when the phone rang.

Emily's face must have mirrored her puzzlement, because Terri mouthed the words, "Who is it?"

Emily shrugged as she once again responded, "Yes, this is Emily Hartman."

"Congratulations, Emily! This is Rockin' Robin from station KLRA, Little Rock's adult rock station, and I've got some fantastic news for you!" he enthused. "You are the lucky winner of our fantastic 'Win a Date with a Star' contest! What do you have to say about that, Emily Hartman?"

The first thought that crossed her mind was to say that she wasn't hard-of-hearing, but she decided against it. Perhaps all radio people spoke in that hearty, ear-splitting tone. Since she never listened to that particular station, she had no way of knowing if he was typical of the breed.

Realizing she had to make some response, she said, "I'm afraid there's been some mistake. I don't know—"

"I know you're overwhelmed, Emily!" he shouted. "And who can blame you? Just sit tight, and let me give you some idea of the magnificent prize you've just won simply by sending in your name, address and telephone number on a postcard."

"But I never sent anyone a postcard, Mr. Robin. I don't even listen to—"

Emily paused because Terri had leaped from her chair and was suddenly making violent arm motions to get her attention. She certainly succeeded. Emily forgot what she was going to say.

Terri whispered, "Is that KLRA calling? Are they saying you won? This is unbelievable!"

Emily stared at her sister as though she had suddenly broken out with a multicolored skin disease. Covering the mouthpiece of the phone, Emily whispered back, "Do you know what's going on?"

"I sent your name in, Emily." Terri's voice rose from whispered excitement to hand-clapping glee. "Find out the details."

"Ms. Hartman, are you there?" came the voice from the phone. "I'm sure the excitement of winning has overwhelmed you for the moment."

"Uh, yes, you could say that," she managed to respond, continuing to eye her sister with a growing sense of horror. "What exactly have I won, did you say?"

He laughed. "As if you didn't know all about the biggest promotional contest this radio station has ever had!" Robin enthused. "You, my dear Ms. Hartman, have won an all-expense-paid trip to Las Vegas, which will include luxury accommodations at one of Las Vegas's finest casino hotels. You will be furnished with a chauffeured limousine and—" His dramatic pause must have been to play up the suspense, Emily decided. Surely he didn't always talk this way. "What every woman in the area would die for! You have a date to spend an evening with Jeremy Jones!"

Emily might never have heard of Rockin' Robin, she might be only vaguely familiar with radio station KLRA, but she would have to be deaf and blind not to know who Jeremy Jones was.

Jeremy Jones had appeared in the music world over a decade before, soared to the top of the music charts with one hit after the other, and had become something of an institution in Las Vegas, appearing there regularly.

And she had a date with him?

There must be some mistake.

"I'm sorry, Mr. Robin, but I'm afraid I can't accept the—"

Terri grabbed the phone out of her hand and said, "Hi, Rockin'. This is Terri Thompson, Emily's sister. She's in shock at the marvelous news." Terri pushed Emily away as she tried to regain the phone. "If you'll just explain to me what Emily needs to do to collect the prize, I'll see that she does it." Her militant glare at Emily made it clear she was prepared to enforce her words.

Perhaps I am *in shock,* Emily admitted to herself, sinking back into the kitchen chair she'd occupied earlier. *Either that or I'm having some sort of a dream. But Jeremy Jones never figured into any of my dreams before!*

She stared at her sister, who was making rapid notes on the back of the envelope that contained Emily's phone bill. Terri was nodding her head vigorously from time to time and uttering affirmative noises into the telephone.

Terri's animation was unfeigned and typical of her nature. There had been times in her life when Emily had envied her older sister's ability to accept life as it came, with arms wide open. The five-year difference in their ages, as well as their contrasting personalities, made a significant difference in their approaches to life.

Terri and Emily had grown up in the public eye as daughters of a state political figure. Terri had accepted the attendant publicity during her growing years with aplomb; handling people with ease; enjoying the verbal sparring; amused at the newspaper, radio and television coverage.

Emily had always disliked the publicity. A shy child, she had hated the attention, the invasive questions, the bulbs flashing, the public speculation regarding her family. In an effort to guard her privacy, Emily had become more introverted as she grew older.

Terri had married Mike Thompson very young, too eager to experience life to waste time on higher education. Emily, on the other hand, had enjoyed school and its comforting schedules. She knew what was expected of her and drew a sense of security from the unvarying routine.

And yet—for all their differences—Terri and Emily were close. Emily knew that Terri loved her. In fact, Terri had insisted, after their parents' death a few years ago, that Emily invest some of her inheritance in the house next door to Terri and Mike. As soon as Terri had heard that her neighbors were being transferred, she had called Emily with the news, pointing out all the advantages of living near each other.

Emily had agreed and had never regretted the move. She adored Patti, her four-year-old niece, and she enjoyed the routine she and Terri had evolved of spending a half hour or so each afternoon, visiting over coffee after Emily arrived home from work.

Emily also enjoyed her career. She'd discovered the soothing predictability of mathematics during her time in school. Now she was part of the accounting department of a nationally known company and felt at home with her responsibilities and duties.

Her life was exactly the way she wanted it—safe and secure. So what in heaven's name could Terri be thinking of, entering her in a contest for a date with Jeremy Jones? How absurd. Emily could think of nothing less appealing than to spend an evening with someone who was so enamored of publicity that he'd be a part of such a gimmicky, ridiculous idea.

Emily watched as Terri concluded the phone call, hung up the phone and let out a tremendous whoop. "You won! I never believed it would happen. I entered your name as a joke, really, never dreaming that—" She came to an abrupt halt and stared at her sister who was watching her warily. "Come on, Emily, aren't you even the least bit excited? I certainly would be."

"I believe you," Emily pointed out dryly. "Now, if you'll explain to me what's going on, perhaps I can share some of your enthusiasm."

Terri stopped her sudden jig and stared at Emily for a moment, then sighed. "Somehow I rather doubt it." She smiled fondly at her sister. "But I'm not going to give up hope on you." Sinking back into a chair, Terri shook her head. "You know, I really worry about you at times."

"Why?" Emily asked in surprise.

"Because you've settled into such a boring routine. You don't seem to be interested in getting out and enjoying yourself at all. You're content to work each day and come home. You spend your evenings and weekends puttering in the garden, curled up with a book, baby-sitting with Patti." She gazed at Emily with concern. "You're too young to be content with such a life. Where's the fun in it?"

Emily smiled. "I happen to consider all of those activities fun. I'm not interested in excitement like you are, Terri."

"I realize there's nothing wrong with those things—in moderation. In fact, they'd be a great way to spend your time, if you were in your sixties!" Terri leaned forward earnestly. "Listen to me. You need to loosen up, do something crazy." She threw her arms out wide. "There's a wonderful world out there, just waiting for you."

Emily smiled at her sister's habit of exaggeration. "I hardly think the world is holding its collective breath for me."

Terry waved her hand dismissively. "You know what I mean. You've done so little for yourself. You've always been so serious about everything—ever since you were a little girl! Whether it was school or your job, you attacked it with grim determination." She leaned back in her chair. "When was the last time you had a date?"

Emily flushed. "I haven't had time to go out with anyone."

"Is that what you tell a man when he asks?"

"I'm not sure how to break the news to you, Terri, but no one has been beating down my door, insisting on spending time with me." Emily smiled. "Let's face it. I've never had your open and outgoing personality. Men don't notice me."

"Of course they notice you. You're very attractive, even though you do nothing to play up your appearance.'' She studied Emily for a moment, as though examining a painting in a museum. ''You have the most gorgeous black hair, you know. It's so dramatic with your ivory complexion. I've always envied you that clear, translucent look.'' Terri rubbed her freckled cheek ruefully. ''You can't tell me men don't notice you. They aren't blind.''

''I work around men every day. Believe me, none of them are interested in me.''

''That's because you never show any interest in them. Don't you understand that a man needs a little encouragement in order to risk a possible rejection?'' Still studying Emily, Terri narrowed her eyes slightly. ''Of course, you don't help yourself by the way you dress.''

Emily glanced down at her tailored skirt and the blouse she had worn underneath her suit jacket. ''What's wrong with the way I dress?'' she demanded.

''Not a thing,'' Terri assured her hastily. ''You always look neat and businesslike. But there are other colors besides black, blue, gray and brown.''

Emily widened her eyes in mock astonishment and gazed at the multicolored sundress Terri was wearing. ''Surely not, Terri! Whatever is the world coming to?''

Terri shook her head but couldn't hide her grin. ''All right. So maybe I've always gone a little overboard with my choice of color, but color is very important. It can change your mood, cheer you up, help you to loosen up and live a little. It helps you to make a statement about yourself.''

''My clothes make a statement about me.''

Terri sighed. "They certainly do. What do you think I'm complaining about? I want you to get out of your rut and begin to live a little."

"And you think a date with Jeremy Jones is the answer?"

Terri grinned. "Well, it certainly won't hurt, little sister! What an opportunity. Any woman in the world would gladly change places with you now, just to have the chance to meet Jeremy Jones in person."

"Fine. Let someone else go to Las Vegas, then."

"No way. You won, and I want you to accept the prize."

"But I can't. I have to work. Plus I have—"

"Will you stop with the silly excuses? Everyone is entitled to a vacation, and you rarely take time off. When you do, you insist on taking Patti and spend most of your free time entertaining her."

Emily knew from experience that arguing with Terri was an exercise in futility. Her sister could always marshal all her facts and figures and generally managed to go for the jugular whenever possible. "You must have been great in debate class," Emily muttered.

Terri looked surprised. "As a matter of fact, I did enjoy it, but I don't see what that has to do with your going to Las Vegas."

Emily sighed. "I have a feeling it has a great deal to do with it. If I can't find a way to convince you that my life is perfectly all right and that I won't go into some sort of decline unless I have a date with Jeremy Jones, you'll have me packed and on my way immediately."

Terri sat back in her chair and folded her arms. "All right. Explain to me why you shouldn't go." Her implacable gaze met Emily's.

Emily stared back for several minutes in silence. Finally she said, "Well, because that contest was offered to some young person who—"

"You're young."

"Terri, I'll be thirty years old in December. That is not considered young."

"Well, it certainly isn't considered retirement age by any stretch of the imagination."

"They expected to have teenagers enter the contest. Young women who were—"

"What nonsense. No teenager could possibly appreciate Jeremy Jones's talent. Why, the man's a genius. He writes his own songs, plays a multitude of instruments and has a voice that causes shivers up and down your spine. This is a fantastic opportunity to visit with an unusual, really fascinating personality."

"I thought I read somewhere that he was married. Isn't he?"

"Who knows? And who cares? This is not a contest to fly to Las Vegas and *marry* Jeremy Jones, for heaven's sake. You're to spend an evening with him. You know—" she waved her hands energetically "—dinner, a show, maybe a party or two, dancing."

"All of that in one evening? He'll have to have more stamina than I have."

"Emily!" Terri shook her head in disgust. "Sometimes I wonder why I even try to help you."

Emily studied her sister's face and smiled. Terri's freckles and sandy-red hair were known throughout the neighborhood. There wasn't a person in town who hadn't been made to feel special because of Terri's personal interest in everyone's well-being. Emily knew that she was fortunate to have Terri as her sister, but she couldn't resist teasing her a little.

"Why me, Terri? Why didn't you send Mrs. Goodman's name in?"

Terri laughed. "Because Mr. Goodman would have pitched a fit if she'd won. She would never be able to convince him that she wasn't having a clandestine affair with good ole Jeremy."

They burst out laughing at her words. No one had ever understood why the elderly Mr. Goodman was so jealous about his equally aging wife, who seemed to be afraid of her own shadow.

"I thought of you, my dearest of all sisters, because I love you and want the best for you. This will give you an opportunity to meet a new type of people; learn about a totally different world from ours. Doesn't that appeal to you at all?" she asked, her tone almost pleading.

"Dearest of all sisters?" Emily repeated, ignoring the rest. "Terri, let's face it, I'm your *only* sister, and sometimes I wonder if that's true. We're too different to actually be related to each other."

"Of course we're sisters. I resemble Mother, and you are the spitting image of Dad's sister. Unfortunately I think you may have inherited some of Aunt Tabitha's traits, as well. Surely you don't want to spend your life the way she did, do you? She spent most of her life alone except for a half dozen cats. You need to get out more, have fun, learn to relax."

"Learn to relax? And you consider an evening with Jeremy Jones relaxing? I wouldn't have the faintest idea what to do or say to the man."

"If it were me, I'd just enjoy sitting there and looking at him. Don't you find him attractive?"

"I never gave him a thought."

Terri's eyes softened, and she gazed out the window with a dreamy expression. "Well, I have. I love the way his tawny-colored hair falls across his forehead in waves. And his eyes. The way they sparkle and shine when he's on television, as though they reflect every light in the room. And that smile! My lord, if the man smiled at me like that, I'd melt in a puddle right at his feet."

"How does Mike feel about this crush you seem to have developed on a star?"

Terri laughed. "It isn't a crush, I assure you. I just appreciate looks, talent and intelligence when I see it."

"How do you know he's so intelligent? By the way his hair curls over his forehead, or the sparkle in his eyes?" Emily's tone was gently mocking.

With prim dignity, Terri replied, "I read an in-depth interview with him that was published in one of the national magazines a few months ago. He was friendly and open, and showed a great deal of insight regarding his life, his career and his future. He didn't take the fame and glory seriously, and made it clear he saw himself as a composer, then a musician, and then an entertainer." She smiled, remembering something. "And he has a great sense of humor. You're going to love him. I just know it."

"If I ever meet him."

"You are going to meet him because you know that I'm right. You're just too stubborn to admit it." Glancing over at the calendar that hung over the table, she said, "Now, then. When do we go shopping?"

"Shopping for what?"

"You certainly don't intend to fly to Las Vegas wearing one of your office uniforms, do you? They probably wouldn't let you off the plane."

"Terri, I have not agreed to go," Emily pointed out firmly.

"But you will," Terri said with the authority that comes with having been the oldest. "And you will be eternally grateful to me for insisting that you take a chance with your life. Just wait and see."

Jeremy Jones stood up from the small table near the piano and stretched. He felt good about the melody he'd found to go with the words that had been running around his head for weeks. Sometimes he hated his ability to write songs, because they hammered at him incessantly, demanding to be set on paper, then later to be matched with a melody.

Now that he had completed this one, perhaps he could get some rest from his subconscious.

Shoving his hands into his pockets, he walked over to the wide expanse of glass that separated the study of his home from the immaculately groomed golf course nearby. The view, as usual, soothed him.

He found the mountains that surrounded Las Vegas fascinating. They were ever-changing in color, depending on how the light reflected off them. The mountains held a sense of timelessness that helped him keep his life in perspective.

The mountains looked down at the splashy glitter and gaudy display that made up the Strip area of the city, no doubt amused at the intrigue, politics and power struggles going on. What would all the plotting, planning and efforts to make it to the top matter in another fifty years or so? The mountains would continue to stand silently and witness the foolish scramble that humans seemed intent to play out.

"Mail call, Jeremy. Looks like we've got a winner!"

Jeremy turned away from the window and faced his business manager, Henry Taylor. Henry generated enough energy and enthusiasm for half a dozen people. Jeremy sometimes felt as though a whirlwind had blown through whenever Henry was around.

"You mean you won a magazine sweepstakes?" Jeremy queried facetiously.

"Not me. You. You're the prize, and we've got ourselves a winner."

Jeremy abruptly sat down in the chair behind his desk. He had a sinking feeling he wasn't going to like what he was about to hear. "*I* am the prize? I don't know what you're talking about."

"Of course you do. I told you about it weeks ago. Had this great idea for a promotion, don't you remember? Down in the South. Thought it would update your image a little. There's a whole new generation out there, and they need to get to know you."

Jeremy leaned back in his chair and wearily shook his head. "No, you never told me about it."

Henry ran his hand over his receding hairline, then sank into the chair in front of Jeremy's desk. "Are you sure? I know that I must have—" He paused as Jeremy continued to shake his head. "Oh. Well, we had this promotion going in Little Rock, Arkansas and—"

"Why Little Rock, Henry? Why not Chicago, Atlanta or Dallas?"

"Because you're doing great in those areas. It's the more rural areas that needed to be beefed up, don't you know?"

Jeremy studied his manager for a moment in silence. Henry Taylor had saved Jeremy's neck a few years ago by coming in and straightening out his finances. Jeremy hadn't understood the business world, nor had he understood the entertainment world. All he knew was music. All he had ever cared about was music—creating it on various instruments, re-creating it in song, expressing himself in the only way he knew.

If it hadn't been for Henry, Jeremy would be teaching music somewhere and playing his compositions at faculty soirees.

Jeremy owed Henry a great deal. Henry was scrupulously honest and had made certain that no one took advantage of Jeremy during their years together. Jeremy respected Henry, but sometimes wondered how it had happened that Henry seemed to run his life.

Such as now.

"All right, Henry. What sort of prize am I?" There was no reason to get upset until he had more details, Jeremy reasoned.

"One of the local stations ran a contest—a 'win a date with a star' thing. You wouldn't believe the response they got! Really sensational."

"Win a date with a star?" Jeremy echoed. "You mean I've got to go to Little Rock and be somebody's escort for the evening?"

"No, nothing like that," Henry hastily assured him. "We're flying her out here."

Jeremy leaned forward and stared at his manager in disbelief. "Are you saying that you are flying some woman all the way from Little Rock to Las Vegas for an evening with me?"

Henry beamed. "You got it."

"Are you out of your mind?" Jeremy's voice had dropped slightly, but the words were clearly enunciated.

Some of Henry's enthusiasm seemed to desert him. "What's wrong?"

"Henry, you know very well that I'm in a very delicate position, trying to get custody of Michelle from Linda. And now you're doing a huge promotion about importing women for me to date?"

"Jeremy, nobody's going to think this is anything but a publicity stunt, which it is. Some young fan of yours is going to come out here, dazzled by Las Vegas and the chance to see you. She'll go back home and tell all her friends how wonderful you are, and they'll buy all your new releases."

Once again Jeremy leaned back in his chair. This time he closed his eyes. He'd been working too hard. Two shows a night, six nights a week. Rehearsals during the day for the new songs, and trying to do the musical score for a movie.

Henry didn't know about the movie or about Jeremy's efforts to find a niche in a related field. Henry didn't know how ready Jeremy was to chuck the whole scene and walk away. He was tired. Tired of working, tired of fighting with Linda, tired of keeping up with new trends.

And now this.

Slowly he opened his eyes and looked at Henry, who sat across from him, anxiously waiting for a response. "All right, Henry. Are you saying that someone won the contest in Little Rock?"

His mild tone seemed to reassure Henry. He bobbed his head energetically. "Yes." He picked up a letter from the stack of mail he'd been carrying. "Emily Hartman is the lucky winner. Now all we have to do is make the arrangements."

"I'm sure you have something in mind."

Henry grinned. "I certainly do. We're going to meet her at the airport with cameras and television. You'll greet her by giving her a bouquet of roses—" He paused when he thought he heard Jeremy say something. "What did you say?"

"Nothing," Jeremy murmured. "Not a thing." He waved his hand. "Go on."

"She'll be taken to one of your rehearsals. She'll also be given a tour of the city—" He stopped when he glanced at Jeremy's expression. "What's wrong with that?"

Jeremy shook his head. "What is there to show of Las Vegas? A ride along the Strip, pointing out casinos?"

"So, what's wrong with that? She's probably never been out here before. Just because you're used to it, doesn't mean everyone is."

"Go on."

Henry consulted his notes. "We thought we'd treat her to a day of beauty at one of the local salons, you know, glamorize her a little, maybe find her a special gown to wear, and then—" he paused, throwing out his hand "—the big event, an evening with you."

Jeremy grinned. "No doubt she can hardly wait."

Henry nodded complacently. "You'd better believe it. We'll give her a Cinderella evening that she can tell her grandchildren about. I wouldn't be surprised if Emily Hartman has been so excited since she won, she hasn't been able to sleep! She probably considers herself to be one very lucky lady!"

Two

What am I getting myself into?'' Emily asked herself out loud the night before she was to fly to Las Vegas. Almost every article of clothing she owned was spread around her bedroom. She was trying to decide what to pack.

Once again Terri had proved to be correct—all her clothes were extremely dull and boring, particularly for Emily's idea of Las Vegas. Admittedly her ideas were sketchy. She'd seen some movies and television shows that had been filmed there. She had an image of noise and confusion, flashy, good-looking show girls, and men with money to throw around.

How could she possibly blend into that scenario? She could wear her wardrobe to a PTA convention and feel right at home.

Why had she agreed to go, anyway? Emily asked herself as she studied her wardrobe critically. In all honesty, she had found it easier to agree to go than to have to come up with new and different excuses whenever Terri brought the trip up in their conversations. Terri was as tenacious as a bulldog, and Emily knew she'd never hear the end of it if she didn't agree to the trip.

Not that she minded a chance to get away from her routine and see another part of the country. On the contrary, Emily had to agree with Terri that her lifestyle was rather sedate. However, Las Vegas wouldn't have been her choice of a place to visit.

As for spending an evening with Jeremy Jones... Emily glanced at the giant poster that Terri had hung on the wall of her bedroom in an effort to promote the star's charm. It was a close-up of Jeremy at a concert, a mike clutched in his hand. She wandered over to the wall and stared at the picture for a moment. Jeremy *was* attractive. In fact, Emily found that particular expression—one of intensity, and yet with a touch of humor in the curve of his mouth—rather intriguing. His eyes were dark in the picture and filled with expression.

A peculiar feeling settled in her stomach. She was going to meet this man within twenty-four hours. What a strange sensation that was. She felt like such a fraud. How could she explain to him that she hadn't entered the contest, that she rarely, if ever, listened to his music, and that she was far from being a typical fan of such a popular entertainer.

However, it was too late to back out. She was committed to go and face whatever happened.

She glanced around in disgust at the clothes she'd laid out. Why had she stubbornly resisted Terri's efforts to go shopping? Her silly pride had really backed her into a corner this time. She had no choice but to pack her tailored clothes and hope for the best.

She found one dress that might be suitable, but she'd had it for a couple of years. Its classic lines and cream color were attractive, but hardly show stopping. She shrugged. There was really no choice—it would have to do.

After filling her suitcase, she closed and placed it on the floor. So much for that. Now all she had to do was to try to get some sleep.

Someday she and Terri would be able to laugh about her nervousness, but at the moment she found nothing amusing about it.

When Emily left the jetway and entered the arrival area of the Las Vegas airport, she was amazed at the crowd swarming around. There seemed to be some commotion: people were waving and talking.

Then a young woman ahead of Emily said, "Jeremy! Jeremy Jones!" in an excited tone. The people between them moved away, and Emily was given a ringside seat of what happened next.

The woman, in a short skirt and with long blond hair, went running up to the man whose picture had hung on Emily's wall for the past couple of weeks. He was easy to identify.

Jeremy wore black pants and a black silk shirt. The neckline was open, revealing his tanned chest. He stood there holding a single rose, and when the young woman ran up to him, he gave her the rose and, leaning over, kissed her on the cheek.

She threw her arms around him. "I can't believe it!" she said, pulling away and staring up at him in awe. "Nobody back home is going to believe that I saw Jeremy Jones as soon as I got off the plane in Vegas." She whirled around and called, "Can you believe it, Judy? And look! He gave me a rose."

Bulbs had been flashing, and several people clustered around the celebrity, asking questions of both him and the woman who was still draped around his neck.

Emily heard an older man's voice rising to be heard over the confusion. "Are you Emily Hartman?" She realized that all the commotion had been meant for her. Her heart sank.

What had she expected? The whole trip was a promotion to give the singer publicity. How could she have been so naive as to expect that she might be treated with a little dignity?

Edging out of the way of the passengers coming off the plane behind her, Emily decided to watch the little drama of mistaken identities being played out in front of her.

The young blond-headed girl looked around at the older man. "I don't know any Emily Hartman. I'm Sally Ann Sherman from Denton, Texas." She turned back to Jeremy and smiled. "I've been a fan of yours ever since I was a little girl."

Emily grinned at Jeremy's flinch. Not that he was so old. She decided, he was probably in his mid-thirties. But this young lady couldn't be much over eighteen.

"Uh, Henry," Emily heard him say to the older man by his side. "There seems to have been some mistake." He began to tug the young woman's arms from around his neck. "I'm sorry, Sally. I thought you were someone else."

She pouted at him prettily. "Won't I do just as well?" she asked coyly.

He grinned. "I'm sure you would. However—" he glanced around at the crowd that had gathered "—I'm looking for Emily Hartman."

Emily watched his gaze slide past her, and she knew that he would never be able to identify her in the crowd. Since she hadn't come to Las Vegas in order to play hide-and-seek, she might as well get on with the next stage of this farce.

Stepping forward, she said quietly, "I'm Emily Hartman."

Both men turned and stared at her. Whatever they had been expecting, Emily certainly wasn't it. The older man's mouth opened a couple of times in silence before he said, "From Little Rock?"

She nodded. "That's right."

Jeremy's mind had gone blank. The impetuous teenager who had thrown herself into his arms had been more or less what he had been expecting; this dignified woman defied all description of what he'd imagined one of his fans to look like.

She was dressed in a cream-colored suit that enhanced a slender, trim body, her black blouse the same color as her hair, which was parted in the middle and pulled to the nape of her neck. Her skin was as pale as alabaster, and her eyes looked almost purple, they were so blue.

This was Emily Hartman? She looked as though she'd just stepped out of a convent.

"You're Emily Hartman?" Jeremy heard Henry repeat in disbelief.

"She's already said she was, Henry," Jeremy said. Stepping forward, he said, "I apologize for the mix-up. You see, we thought—"

"I'm very aware of what you thought, Mr. Jones," she said in a cool tone. She glanced around at the group of people who were watching them. "I suppose all of this—" she waved her hand at a couple of photographers and a man carrying a small video recorder "—is for my benefit?"

She didn't have to sound so damned bored, Jeremy thought with irritation. After all, she was the one who had been so eager to win a trip to meet him.

"Yes, it is. However, we didn't expect someone like—" He paused, trying to think of a tactful way to phrase what he was thinking. "I mean, usually my fans are dressed a little more, uh . . ."

When he seemed to be at a loss for words, she said, "Yes, I'm certain I'm not dressed in a way that is similar to your fans, Mr. Jones. But then again—" her glance slid over the open collar of his shirt, then down to his hands and the rings he wore "—you're wearing enough jewelry for both of us, aren't you?"

Jeremy heard Henry's gasp just as another flash went off. All he could think about was getting out of there. Obviously Ms. Emily Hartman was less than impressed with their planned welcome. He wasn't sure what her problem was, but frankly he didn't need the aggravation.

"Well, so much for formalities," he said, trying to hide his irritation. "Welcome to Las Vegas." Taking her by the shoulders, he steadily lessened the distance between them. Suddenly changing his intent to kiss her chastely on the cheek, Jeremy found her mouth with his. He felt her stiffen, but he refused to release her, taking a rather grim pleasure in behaving in a way that he knew she would find offensive.

When he raised his head, he found himself staring down into darkly fringed pools of shocked surprise. Her eyes fascinated him, particularly now when they began to flash with anger.

"What do you think you're—" she began, trying to move away from him.

He turned her so that he had one arm around her shoulders and began to walk down the concourse. "If you'll give your ticket to Henry, he'll have your bags picked up and taken to your hotel room. In the meantime, I need to get to rehearsal."

"But I don't need—"

"We thought you might enjoy seeing a rehearsal, and then Henry has plans for you to be shown some of the sights while I get ready for my early show."

While he was talking, Jeremy kept moving rapidly down the concourse, so that Emily had to run to keep up with him. Several people waved and called his name, but he kept his attention on her. As soon as they reached the front doors of the terminal, a limousine pulled up in front of them.

Jeremy helped her into the limousine and quickly got in behind her. Settling beside her, he glanced over at her and shook his head. "So, what's going on?"

Emily felt a little dazed. She had practically run the length of the airport and was only now able to catch her breath. "What do you mean?"

"C'mon, lady. The joke's over. What's with the nun's habit and hairdo? What are you doing out here in Las Vegas?"

Nun's habit and hairdo? Was he making fun of her? Granted, she might not look like a Las Vegas show girl, but she certainly wasn't dressed to be held up to ridicule.

"I am here at your invitation," she managed to say stiffly.

"Hardly. I didn't have anything to do with this whole mess."

"Mess?"

"Promotion...gimmick...hoopla. You know. 'Win a Date with a Star' thing." He studied her for a moment. "Why in the world would someone like you enter such a contest?"

"Someone like me?" she asked faintly.

He grinned. "You'd probably be much happier staying at home knitting and talking to your cat."

Shades of Aunt Tabitha! Perhaps Terri had a point after all.

"For your information, I don't knit, nor do I have a cat."

He shrugged. "Just a figure of speech. You don't look like the kind of person who enters contests."

"I'm not. And I don't."

"Now we're getting somewhere. So what's going on? Why are you pretending to be Emily Hartman?"

Emily could feel anger stirring somewhere deep inside. Since she considered herself to be a rather calm and placid person, this new emotion unnerved her. "I am not pretending. My name *is* Emily Hartman." She gave him a cool stare. "Would you care to see some identification?"

He met her stare calmly. "No, I'll take your word for it."

"Thank you very much," she said in her most icy tones.

"Why'd you enter the contest?"

"I didn't."

"Oh?"

"My sister entered my name."

"Why in the world would she do such a thing?"

"A very good question, Mr. Jones. You'd have to know Terri to appreciate the way her mind works. I'm not sure I could possibly explain in a way that you'd understand."

He'd once had a tutor who spoke to him in such precise tones, and Jeremy found himself grinning. Folding his arms, he settled back into his seat and said, "Try."

She stared at him in silence for a moment. Emily was unnerved at how attractive she found the man— gold rings and all. His eyes danced like an ebony fire. She found his amusement disconcerting, as though she were the butt of a joke that she wasn't able to comprehend.

"It's not important. She entered my name, and I won."

"Why did you come? It's obvious you aren't one of my fans."

She glanced at him in surprise. "What makes you say that?"

"You aren't the type."

"And exactly what type of person would be a fan of yours?"

He thought about that for a moment. "Oh, a little more laid-back, maybe. A little less formal. Someone who doesn't take herself quite so seriously."

"Is that what you think about me?"

"Frankly, I don't have the foggiest idea what to think about you, Ms. Hartman. All I know is that I've got a rehearsal to attend." The car had pulled up in front of a large casino. "You can either come in with me, or I can have you taken over to your hotel. Whatever you want to do."

Emily felt shaken to the core. She had never realized that her shyness and her lack of social repartee came across as stiff and uptight. Was that why people generally left her alone? Was she really as priggish as he'd implied?

"I'd like to attend your rehearsal," she said quietly, trying to find some way of explaining herself to him.

He shrugged. "Suit yourself." Stepping out of the car, he held out his hand to her. "I've got to hurry.

The band's been waiting for me for almost half an hour. Their time is my money.''

Taking her elbow, he hurried her through the door.

Emily couldn't seem to take in all the sights and sounds that filled the mammoth room they traversed. Giant chandeliers hung along the expansive ceiling, while below, noisy slot machines and various tables covered in green were the focus of several people.

Jeremy waved to the man who stood in front of the door to the showroom. "How's it goin', Eric?"

"Not too bad, Jeremy. Not too bad."

They slipped inside, and Emily found herself in another large room, filled with empty tables and chairs and dominated by a stage. The curtains were open, and several people wandered around on the stage. Sounds of music from various instruments echoed in the room.

Someone up on the platform spotted them. "There he is! It's about time you showed up," came a loud call.

The drummer beat out a saucy rhythm, and someone laughed.

Jeremy dropped her arm. "Just find a seat out here. I'll see you later." Walking down to the front, he vaulted onto the stage amid catcalls and jokes.

Emily became engrossed watching the professional musicians do what they do so well. She was amazed at the effort expended on each song. They worked well together, despite the casual attitude toward one another. Watching Jeremy Jones at work was different from what she had expected.

What, exactly, had she expected?

She had assumed that he would be arrogant and egotistical. Wasn't that the image most entertainers had? She'd expected him to be insulted by her little dig about his jewelry. If it had bothered him, he hadn't shown it. Emily realized that she envied him his self-possession.

Jeremy Jones appeared to be comfortable with who he was. He wasn't trying to impress anyone, despite what she had fully believed she would find when she met him. And from where she sat watching, there was no denying his talent. His voice had a full, rich quality that kept chills running up and down her spine. At one point he walked out toward the empty room as though singing directly to her, a half smile on his face.

She found herself blushing because the song was definitely a love song, and he sang the words as though he'd written them especially for her.

"Ms. Hartman?" a voice said beside her.

Emily jumped and was embarrassed to be found so engrossed in Jeremy's singing. She turned and saw a beautiful young woman standing there. "Yes?"

"Hi, I'm Cynthia Taylor. My dad's Jeremy's business manager. He thought you might be tired and want to go to your hotel now."

Emily glanced at her watch, amazed to see how much time had passed since she had arrived. Looking up at the stage, she could tell that Jeremy was deeply involved in what the band was presently doing. Nodding her head, she stood and followed the woman out of the room. At the doorway, she looked back in time to see Jeremy glance up and see her. He gave her a wave and blew her a kiss, which caused a cacophony of whistles, blasts on the horns and a roll of the drums from the band.

"They're like a bunch of little boys," Cynthia explained with a grin. "It's hard to believe they're all supposed to be grown men."

Cynthia and Emily walked across the large entrance of the hotel once more. "I don't know why they didn't put you up in this hotel, but I think you'll enjoy your rooms at—" she named another famous casino hotel that Emily had noticed on the way from the airport. Cynthia pointed to a limousine that was waiting for them, and Emily wanted to laugh. She'd never seen so many long, sleek automobiles gathered in one place, before coming to this glittery town.

"We thought you might want to spend the evening getting used to the change in time, because tomorrow we have a big day planned for you."

Emily smiled at the younger woman. "That sounds fine with me. I'm a little overwhelmed at the moment. Everything is so different here."

Cynthia laughed. "I know. But I really love it. The air is so clean and at least at this time of year, pleasantly cool. Of course the summer months get a little warm, but I wouldn't want to live anywhere else."

Emily looked at her in surprise. "But don't you travel with Jeremy?"

Cynthia shook her head. "Oh, no. Mom and I live here all the time. Actually Jeremy's cut back on his tours in the past few years. And I suppose he'll be staying in one place permanently if—" She stopped as though suddenly aware of what she was saying. "I'm sorry. I didn't mean to bore you with Jeremy's personal affairs.''

Emily didn't want to embarrass the young woman by admitting that she was enjoying the conversation. So Jeremy might stay in one place permanently. Why? And what would that do to his career? And would he choose to live in Las Vegas all the time? And what difference could it possibly make to her?

"Here we are," Cynthia announced brightly, a few minutes later.

Emily recognized the famous hotel from various television shots she'd seen. She was going to feel like royalty staying there.

On the way upstairs, Cynthia said, "Tomorrow is Jeremy's last show for a few months, so there's going to be a big party at his home later." She opened the door and stepped aside, motioning Emily to enter.

Emily walked in and paused, gazing around in surprise. She stood at the top of three steps that led into a conversational area with sofas and chairs intimately grouped. One wall was glass and looked over an emerald-green golf course.

Turning, Emily noticed that Cynthia had crossed the room to a pair of double doors, which she opened with a flourish. Emily slowly followed her. Inside the room was a bed large enough to sleep six people. The bed was on a dais, with drapes hanging from the ceiling at each corner.

"Unbelievable," Emily murmured.

Cynthia grinned. "I know what you mean. I guess they like to make a splash or something." She glanced around the room. "It looks like you'll have everything you need here."

"I should hope so. My entire house could probably fit into the size of these two rooms!"

She opened a closet door and found that her clothes had been unpacked and hung, her shoes neatly lined up beneath them.

"I almost feel as though I'm dreaming," she said with a glance over her shoulder at Cynthia, "but if so, don't wake me up just yet."

Cynthia laughed. "Wait until you see what's happening tomorrow. They've planned a pamper day at one of the salons here in town."

"A what?" Emily asked, staring at the younger woman.

"You know. You'll spend the day at the salon, and they give you the works—massage, facial, new hairstyle and makeup, manicure—" She waved her hand. "A day of beauty. Then I'm to take you shopping for something really outstanding to wear while you're here—a gown for tomorrow night and another one for your date with Jeremy."

Emily sank down onto the side of the bed. "I had no idea all of that was part of the package."

Cynthia grinned. "To be honest, the pamper day was my idea. Dad was asking me what I would consider a perfect visit to Las Vegas. The date with Jeremy was a brilliant idea, of course, but I'd want all the necessary trimmings to feel that I looked my absolute best, so I mentioned the pamper day idea, and an unlimited charge at one of the boutiques and—"

"And your father agreed?"

"Not right away, of course. He always thinks I'm too extravagant, but Jeremy was there and said if that was my idea of a good time, he was certain one of his fans would enjoy it, as well."

"I see," Emily said faintly. She felt even more of a fraud now. Obviously they were sparing no expense to make her feel comfortable. Glancing in the mirror, she looked at the neat, dignified woman reflected back at her. She doubted very seriously if she could be transformed into a glittering butterfly, no matter what they did.

"I need to run," Cynthia announced, returning to the front room. "I wrote down numbers where you can reach me or Jeremy or Dad. Mother's visiting her sister in Sacramento this week, or you could have met her. I know she would have enjoyed seeing you."

Emily didn't know what to say.

"I'll pick you up in the morning about nine o'clock, if that's all right," Cynthia continued, opening the door.

"That's fine," Emily managed to say before the door closed.

She felt disoriented. Glancing around the room once again, she wondered what she was doing there and how she'd ever allowed Terri to talk her into going to Vegas.

Obviously the plan had been for someone Cynthia's age to win the contest. Cynthia couldn't be over twenty years old. She made Emily feel old enough to be her mother. But there was little that Emily felt she could do about the situation now.

And a date with Jeremy Jones, as well?

She recalled what he'd looked like at the airport and later, during rehearsals. She knew that under ordinary circumstances he wouldn't have ever noticed her.

Nevertheless, she would now be moving in his circles, at least for the next few days.

"Well, Cinderella, here you are," she murmured to herself when she walked into the luxurious bathroom. She felt like a very dowdy Cinderella, expected to impress the prince. Smiling to herself as she began to fill the imposing bathtub with hot water and bath oils, Emily discovered a hitherto-unknown part of her personality surfacing.

"I almost wish I did have a fairy godmother," she decided as she lowered herself into the scented water. "I would show up at his party looking like a knock-out and make him eat his words!" She stretched out in the water so that only her neck and head were above the water. "He's so blasted arrogant and sure of himself. It would be fun to show him that, far from looking like I came from a convent, I could be attractive enough to be in one of the shows here."

She laughed at her absurd notion. In the first place, she didn't have the looks, the height or the poise to be a professional entertainer. "Or the disposition," she added aloud.

Already the ambiance of Las Vegas was beginning to affect her.

Terri had been right when she'd said Emily had really gotten into a rut. Emily was beginning to gain a new sense of freedom since arriving in Las Vegas, a feeling she'd never experienced quite so strongly before. She found it easier to talk to people, even Jer-

emy, than she generally did. And Cynthia treated her
as though they'd known each other for years.

She felt different somehow and wondered what it
would be like if, for just a little while, she were to pretend—like Cinderella—that she *was* someone different. It might be fun to pretend—only for a little while,
of course—that she wasn't shy and boring. Instead she
would be beautiful and full of fun...exciting. Jeremy Jones would be captivated by her charm, en-
chanted by her wit and fascinated by her beauty.

Emily closed her eyes at the thought and smiled—a
rather wicked smile for such a nice young woman.

Three

—

Twenty-four hours later, Emily stood before the full-length mirror in the bedroom of her suite. Never again would she doubt the truth of fairy tales. Obviously, from the view she had in the mirror, her godmother was alive and well, living in Las Vegas, Nevada.

She didn't recognize the woman in the mirror. Peering closer, she studied the eyes gazing back at her. That particular shade of blue was the only thing that looked in the least familiar. Everything else had changed.

The sedate hairdo had disappeared, as had the conservative suit and accessories. The woman in the mirror looked as though she could have stepped from a Fifth Avenue condominium—on her way to a rather fancy ball.

The woman at the salon had complimented her on her wealth of hair and its striking natural color. Since Emily had never given her hair much thought, she was surprised to have someone exclaim over it. After giving the woman permission, Emily watched as she began to cut and thin it, shaping it close to her face in front, allowing the thick tresses at the back of her head to fall to her shoulders.

Removing the weight had given her hair a bounce and waves she'd never known it had. Obviously Terri wasn't the only one in the family to get some curls, even though Emily's hair was tamer than Terri's.

Fascinated by her new look, Emily continued to study her image.

Her face had mysterious highlights and subtle shadows that emphasized the blueness of her eyes, the translucence of her skin, her high cheekbones and slightly indented chin.

The dress sparkled every time she drew breath. Tiny straps held it in place over upthrust breasts, molding to her waist, which looked as though a man's hands could encircle it. The dress skimmed her hips and followed the curve of her thighs. A slit from the floor-length hem to the knee enabled her to walk.

Cinderella had never looked like this! And neither had Emily.

Of course Emily acknowledged that her godmother had taken on the form of Henry Taylor's daughter, Cynthia, and several hours had gone into the transformation. Smiling into the mirror, Emily admitted to herself that the hours had been worth it.

Later she'd been whisked to a shop in one of the malls, where she was handed gown after gown to choose from.

When she had tried on this particular dress—a shimmering white satin—she knew this was the one she had to have. Jeremy Jones could not mistake her for a nun in this outfit.

Turning sideways, she idly noted that the dress faithfully molded her form from every angle. She'd had no idea that she could look quite so provocative. Because of the snug fit of the skirt and the height of the shoes Cynthia had insisted she wear, Emily could only take small, swaying steps, which enhanced the way her body moved.

She laughed out loud. "I love it!" Slowly turning in a circle, she eventually paused in front of the mirror. "Terri, my dear, I think you may have created a monster. I never knew playing dress-up could be so much fun."

She wondered what Jeremy Jones would think if he could see her now. The slow, enticing smile that appeared in the mirror startled her. Emily Hartman had never smiled that way in her life. Perhaps she was bewitched. It would serve Terri right.

The doorbell rang, and she practiced her new way of walking without haste to the door. When she opened it, Henry and Cynthia stood there.

"My God, I don't believe it!" Henry muttered. Both Cynthia and Emily laughed.

"I told you she was something, Dad."

"Come in, both of you."

Henry walked in, never taking his eyes off Emily. "We thought you might join us for dinner before the show. Cynthia said she told you about the party afterward." He glanced around the room. "Is this place all right?"

Emily smiled. "All right? I never knew anyone lived like this. You may have spoiled me for life." She motioned to the table in front of one of the sofas. "The hotel sent up champagne if you'd like to have some."

Henry said, "No, thanks. Not my drink at all. But if you two want any of it, go ahead."

Emily shook her head. "I never got into the habit of drinking, and I figure I'm too old to start now."

Henry looked her up and down. "Cynthia tried to prepare me for the transformation, but I had no idea you would be such a knockout." He walked around her slowly. "Really sensational."

"Do you think Jeremy will recognize me?" she asked with a chuckle.

"Well, of course he— Come to think of it, I'm not so sure he would. He didn't have much time to be with you yesterday, did he?"

"No. And he did have a few pithy comments to make regarding my attire, as I recall."

Cynthia winked at Emily and said to her father, "You know, it would be fun to see if he does recognize her, wouldn't it, Dad? Did you ever tell him that she planned to be there tonight?"

"No, he's been so busy that I really haven't had a chance to talk with him since Emily got here."

"Then let's just not mention to Jeremy that Emily decided to attend, and see if he recognizes her. What do you think?"

Henry shrugged. "It's up to Emily, of course. I had planned to take her backstage between shows." He glanced at her. "Whatever you would like to do is fine with me."

Why not? If she intended to be Cinderella for the evening, she might as well play the part to the hilt. She smiled at Henry. "Actually I think it might be fun. It really won't matter if he recognizes me or not, since our date isn't until tomorrow evening. I would just as soon wait to see him at the party. Even so, he probably won't even notice me."

Both father and daughter broke into laughter. "Oh, he'll notice you," Cynthia finally managed to say. "I just want to see his face when he realizes who you are."

The three of them had an enjoyable dinner, and Emily learned a great deal about the loyalty both of them had to Jeremy.

"He's a musical genius, you know," Henry explained over dessert and coffee. "He taught himself how to play most musical instruments before he was ten, then went on to learn how to read music."

"Did he always want to be an entertainer?" Emily asked.

"Not really, although he has the warm personality for it. He sings with such ease and forms a rapport with the audience that has to be seen to be believed."

"I'm rather surprised that he agreed to this type of promotion," she said.

"I'm afraid I didn't give him much choice. Fortunately he gave in without giving me too much of a hard time."

"You mean he didn't want to spend an evening with a lucky contest-winner?"

"Oh, don't get me wrong. It's just that he doesn't see the need to promote himself."

"But you do."

"It can't hurt. And look at the interest it stirred up. It got your attention, didn't it? I suppose you've always been a fan of his."

Emily discovered that she didn't want to say anything that would make her sound ungrateful. She was aware of how much time and expense had gone into her visit. And yet she couldn't in all honesty state that she was a fan of his.

"Let's just say that I've enjoyed his music, but I never expected to meet him."

"Well, then you'll enjoy his show tonight. That's why we brought you in early enough for his last performance, even though your official date with him isn't until tomorrow night."

"I appreciate the thought. I'm intrigued by all the behind-the-scene work that goes on. I really enjoyed the rehearsal yesterday."

"Jeremy works hard, that's for sure. He's due for some rest and relaxation."

Cynthia, who had remained quiet through most of the meal, spoke up. "He won't have much of that if he wins his custody case."

Her father gave her a scowl that effectively silenced her. He glanced at Emily. "He's been having some problems regarding custody of his daughter."

"Oh. I didn't realize he had any children, although I had heard somewhere that he was married."

"He's divorced. Michelle was barely two when he and Linda split up. That was almost three years ago. Because he was on the road so much, Jeremy agreed that Linda should have custody, but several things have changed since then."

"I'll say," Cynthia agreed, but subsided once again when her father glanced over at her.

Henry checked his watch. "Are you ready to go? The show starts in a few minutes."

The three of them walked through the lobby of the casino hotel together. Emily noticed that she and Cynthia garnered their share of looks as they passed by.

Why, this is fun, she thought to herself. Of course she would never consider dressing like this in real life, but here in Las Vegas, the clothes were part of the fantasy. Adding to the sense of freedom was the fact that no one knew Emily here. As a child she'd been cautioned that her behavior reflected on her father and the family in general.

Perhaps that was why she'd always been so self-conscious.

Here, no one knew who she was, and no one cared. She could do and say whatever she chose.

Henry paused at the doorway of the theater where a young man waited to show them to their seats. Emily was surprised to see how different the room looked lit up at night and filled with people.

She took careful steps as she followed Cynthia down the terraced walkway. Tripping down the stairway was not what she had in mind to be noticed.

They were seated at a curving banquette with room to seat several people. A waiter took their drink orders, and Emily studied the crowd. There was a buzz of excitement, and she could feel the energy building as the time drew near for the show.

The house lights darkened just as the orchestra began to play the song that had become Jeremy's theme song. An unseen announcer welcomed the audience to the show, and the curtain opened. The hushed expectancy in the room caused Emily to hold her breath for a moment.

Then the orchestra changed tempo—this time playing one of Jeremy's recently released songs that had quickly climbed the charts. The voice that had become familiar to millions of people came over the sound system full and strong as large swirls of fog filled the stage.

Out of the fog stepped Jeremy.

Emily was shaken by the illusion for a moment. How had he done that? One moment the stage was occupied by the orchestra; the next moment Jeremy materialized before them. From the soft sounds of awe around her, she realized she wasn't the only one impressed with his entrance.

Jeremy slowly came down a curving ramp until he was on center stage, only a few feet from the footlights, continuing to sing. If she had thought him at-

tractive the day before, he was devastating now, his
charisma surging out into the audience in almost vis-
ible waves.

Within minutes he had the crowd ecstatic. After
each number he chatted with them, greeting people,
asking others where they were from, eliciting laughter
by gently teasing the more gregarious people in the
audience. He appeared sincerely interested in them,
and they responded wholeheartedly.

She tried to concentrate on the music, the songs, the
words—and not on the man—but it was very difficult. Once again he was dressed entirely in black. He
must have known how well it showed off his tan and
his golden brown hair. The material of his shirt glis-
tened under the lights as though wet, and fit his
shoulders as though made for them. Emily smiled at
the thought. No doubt the shirt *had* been custom
made.

She found herself mesmerized by the way he moved
around the stage. He had a pantherish stride that ef-
fortlessly carried him downstage, where he would
crouch and shake someone's hand or whirl and pace
back toward the orchestra. His trousers faithfully followed the contours of his taut and muscled hips and
thighs. Emily found herself fascinated with the way he
moved, the way he wore his clothes, the way he
sounded, the way his smile flashed.

And this was the man she was going to spend tomorrow evening with. Emily would never have admitted to Terri that she was impressed with Jeremy
Jones in any way, but the more she heard about him
and the more she saw of him...the more she realized

that she was in danger of forming a crush on him just like any teenager, which was absolutely ridiculous, she reminded herself.

She was twenty-nine years old and much too mature to fall into the adolescent habit of idolizing some star. But she could certainly understand how people could fall into that trap. What she had to keep reminding herself was that none of this was real—it was all part of her fantasy. She was playing Cinderella all right, but the Prince didn't even know she existed. Hopefully by tomorrow evening she would be her sane and sensible self.

Jeremy closed his show with a rousing number. The audience loved him. They left no doubt in anyone's mind.

"So what do you think?"

Emily glanced around at Henry as though waking up from a dream.

"He's one of a kind," she said, unwilling to admit the effect he'd had on her.

Henry laughed. "You can certainly say that again. Have you changed your mind about going backstage?"

She shook her head. "I don't think so. I'd like to hang on to my illusions for a while longer." She smiled as he escorted her and Cynthia to the car. "I suppose this is all old hat to you."

"Actually I haven't seen his show in a while," Henry admitted ruefully. "I don't attend unless he wants me here for a reason. I spend my evenings with the family."

"It's difficult for me to visualize people living and working in Las Vegas and having a normal home life."

"I'm not surprised," Henry said with a smile. "We don't promote our everyday world. It's too much like everyone else's."

They drove several miles toward the mountains, then pulled up at a gate with a sign that read Spanish Trails Country Club. A gatekeeper saluted them and opened the gate. Inside the walls everything looked lushly green, with colorful flowers bordering the drive. Street lamps made the area as bright as daylight.

When they stopped in front of a building, Emily's first thought was that it was a hotel. Then she realized this must be Jeremy's home. It looked as though it belonged somewhere along the Mediterranean Sea. White stucco walls shone in the reflection of yard lights.

The sight of all the cars parked nearby and the people entering the house gave Emily a sudden feeling of stage fright. She'd never been to a party such as this. Would she be able to handle herself with the grace and style she hoped to portray? For the first time she wondered how Cinderella had ever managed.

Cynthia chatted as they walked up the long driveway to the house, giving the names of some of the owners of the various cars they passed, names of very famous people. Cynthia appeared to take everything in stride.

The place was crowded when they walked in. Emily recognized several faces that she'd seen only in magazines, movies and on television, and a sense of unreality settled over her that never entirely left.

Within minutes after they arrived, Henry had introduced Emily to several people, found her a fruit drink to sip on and excused himself. Emily knew that as far as Henry was concerned, this was still part of his job. Cynthia spied an acquaintance and soon disappeared, but Emily was too busy to allow the fact that she was on her own to unnerve her.

Two of the band members strolled up and began talking with her as though they knew her, but she was confident that they did not remember her from the day before. Names seemed to be unimportant. Everyone joked and chatted, and she began to relax. It was going to be all right. From somewhere deep within, Emily drew on a sense of self-confidence she didn't know she had and found herself returning the quips and teasing with gentle good humor.

By the time Jeremy arrived, Emily felt completely relaxed and at ease.

A crowd gathered around him. Obviously several people had flown into Las Vegas just to attend the party, and there was a great deal of hugs and kisses exchanged between Jeremy and several beautiful women.

"Do you know Jeremy well?" a voice asked. Emily turned around and recognized Jeremy's lead guitarist standing there with a drink in his hand.

She smiled. "Not really. But I'm very impressed."

"Yeah, I know what you mean. I've been with him for years, and he still amazes me." Glancing at her drink, he said, "Can I get you another one?"

"Sure. It's fruit punch."

He grinned. "I'll see what I can find you, pretty lady. Be right back."

How kind of him. She couldn't get used to the instant friendliness of the people. Emily was amused at the way several of the men were treating her, as though she were a mirage and they were afraid to blink in case she disappeared.

"I don't believe we've met."

Emily would recognize that voice now, no matter where she heard it. Slowly turning, she found that a sudden sense of excitement swept over her as she faced Jeremy Jones.

The adrenaline was still bouncing throughout his body. Emily could almost see it pulsating around him. His hair was damp, as though he'd just showered. And he'd changed clothes. This time he was all in white. She couldn't decide which color best suited him.

"We look like a pair that should be on the top of a wedding cake, don't we?" he asked with a grin, taking her hands and holding them out on either side.

She smiled and nodded.

"What's the matter, cat got your tongue?" he asked, leaning over to peer into her face more closely. Drawing back slightly, he said, "I know you, don't I?"

She shrugged.

"Ah. Now I get it. Tonight you are going to be the mystery lady, is that it?"

Emily hadn't been conscious of the fact that she hadn't said anything. Somehow, being with him again had seemed to take her breath away.

Clearing her throat, she managed to say, "I'm not all that mysterious."

He tilted his head slightly, then slowly reached over and picked up a curl that lay on her shoulder. "You are a very beautiful woman. I suppose you know that."

The look he gave her made her feel beautiful. His glowing eyes were filled with appreciation...and something more. She watched the corners of his mouth tilt slightly. "Are you going to tell me your name?"

"Cinderella."

He threw back his head and burst into laughter, causing those nearby to glance around and smile. "Well, Cinderella, welcome to my party. And where is your Prince Charming?" He glanced around the room just as the lead guitarist returned with her drink.

"Aw, c'mon, Jeremy. Don't cut me out with every chick I meet, man. How about a little fair play around here?"

Emily could feel the heat rise in her cheeks.

"Hi, Leon. I didn't realize you brought a date tonight."

"I didn't. I had just met her and was playing the gentleman by getting her a drink."

Jeremy studied Emily in silence for a moment. If Emily hadn't known better, she would have thought that he was looking deep into her soul. Finally he said, "Well, in that case, Leon, I'm afraid you're out of luck tonight. This lady came to see me, and as her host, I find that I must look after her. I certainly can't let a rogue like you take advantage of her."

Placing her hand in the crook of his arm, he said, "I'm very glad you came to my party, Cinderella. Are you going to allow me to be your Prince Charming?"

"Only until midnight."

Glancing at his watch, he laughed. "That's a deal. In the meantime, let me introduce you to some of these people."

Jeremy never once asked her name. Instead, he introduced everyone to her as though she were royalty. She could feel herself falling under his spell, but no longer cared. After all, what could possibly happen at a party? She was safe, and she knew it. Henry was somewhere around. So was Cynthia. She could relax and enjoy the fantasy.

People seemed to accept the fact she was with Jeremy without question, although she received several dirty looks from various women.

He was attentive to her needs, making sure she had something to eat from the buffet, keeping her glass filled, dancing with her. Their conversation was impersonal to a degree. Although he asked no questions about her, he seemed to feel it permissible to pay her outrageous compliments.

Had he recognized her? If so, she could not tell. Gradually she began to realize that he had steadily drawn her out all evening, asking her opinion about movies, books, politics, her hobbies, her favorite color, favorite pastime, favorite food.

Emily felt totally caught up in the fantasy of the evening. He really was being Prince Charming—gracious, caring, teasing, and oh, so very handsome.

As the evening wore on, Emily felt everything going on around her like a dream. Lights and cameras flashed and clicked nearby, and she didn't care. He held her close to him while they danced and at one point hummed a couple of words.

"You have a very nice voice," she whispered rather primly into his ear.

She felt his chest shake and glanced up at him. His face seemed to waver above her. "Thank you very much," he replied solemnly, but she had recognized the chuckle she'd felt more than heard.

"I suppose everyone tells you that." For some reason she was having trouble with her tongue. Although her mind was perfectly clear, her tongue seemed to keep wrapping itself around her teeth.

He pulled her closer and kissed her in front of her ear. "But not with such honest sincerity," he whispered.

Emily relaxed against him. He felt so good to lean against. Suddenly she felt tired. She felt so tired that her feet no longer wanted to move. She sighed and tucked her head under his chin.

"Cinderella?"

"Hmm?"

"How much have you had to drink tonight?"

"Nothing."

She wondered why he chuckled. "Then what was in that glass you just set down before we came out to dance?"

"Fruit punch."

"And?"

"That's all."

"Not likely, darlin'. Those are rum punches you've been putting away all evening."

She pulled away and looked up at him quizzically. "They can't possibly be," she explained with dignity. "You see, I don't drink."

He kept his expression solemn. "I see. Well, that could certainly explain a lot of things, couldn't it?"

She nodded rather emphatically.

"Would you like to go outside for a few minutes, and maybe get some fresh air?"

"Why, is it too hot in here for you?"

"Ahh, yes. I think you could safely say that." Jeremy took her arm and led her out the double doors onto a wide terrace overlooking part of the golf course.

"Oh, how beautiful." Emily thought the moonlight on the carefully manicured grounds made a spectacular picture. She wished she knew how to paint, to get that mystical glow to the night.

"Would you like some coffee?"

She smiled up at him. "No, thank you. I'm fine."

"If you say so."

"You have a wonderful home. It's hard to believe that only one person lives here."

"Oh, I have several people who stay here, some to look after the house and gardens, plus some of the band members come and go. We all treat it like a hotel at times."

"I'm not surprised. Your home is bigger than most governors' mansions," she said, waving toward the door they had recently passed through.

"Are you happy with your life?" he asked softly.

She turned to him and noted how the moonlight burnished the side of his face with a glow. Emily reached up and stroked her finger along his cheek and jawline. "I always thought I was," she said wistfully. "Until now. I never realized there was anyone like you in this whole world."

"There's nothing special about me."

"Oh, but there is," she protested earnestly. "You are so talented. And you're so gentle... and warm... and loving..." Her words faded as she continued to stare up at him. "I have your poster on my bedroom wall," she confessed.

He grinned. "You do? That surprises me a great deal, but I'm gratified."

"Actually, my sister Terri put it there. But I decided I rather liked it, so I left it."

He slid his arms around her waist and pulled her to him gently. "I wonder if you're going to deplore your honesty in the morning."

She looked up at him, puzzled. "You don't think I should have told you about the picture?"

"Oh, I'm extremely pleased that you did. I'm rather amazed to find that I very much want to be considered special by you."

Jeremy leaned down until his mouth touched hers. His lips softly brushed against hers, as though waiting for her to move away or protest. She did neither. She just stood there, staring up at him. Then her heavily fringed eyes closed as she slid her arms around his neck.

This time he kissed her with more assurance, his lips moving over hers, tasting and caressing as he explored the contours of her mouth. Breathless, Emily gasped slightly, and he took advantage of her parted lips to deepen the kiss.

The feelings that rushed over her were so new they took her unaware. Of course she had been kissed. Many times. But no one had caused her to feel as though she'd been swept up into a whirlwind of feeling before.

She enjoyed the way his body pressed so intimately against her own. Her fingers tentatively touched the hair that waved around his ears, then began to explore its soft texture.

He claimed her mouth as though placing his mark of possession on her. And yet for all the urgency she felt in him, Emily was aware of the gentleness there, as well. She knew that all she had to do was to step away from him, and he would let her go. But she wasn't ready to step away. She wanted to go on kissing him, to go on and on until all the world was lost and there were only the two of them, locked in each other's arms.

No wonder Cinderella fell in love with the prince. How could anyone possibly resist his charms?

Four

—

"Good morning."

Emily heard the soft, husky sound of a sleepy male voice somewhere nearby. Very close nearby.

Her head felt as though a battalion of men were inside it, each one equipped with a jackhammer—each one industriously at work, chipping away at her skull.

She lay there, trying to think, trying to come to grips with the various messages her senses were sending to her.

Emily refused to open her eyes. She might never open them again. A stray thought crossed her mind, and she wondered if she was just to continue to lie there, never moving, if eventually someone would assume she had died. Then maybe they would cart her off somewhere. Somewhere private where she could come to terms with what must have happened the night before. If only she could remember...

Even if the gentle voice hadn't spoken, Emily would have known that it was now daylight—the light hitting her tightly closed eyelids was entirely too bright to be caused by artificial means—which meant that midnight had definitely been there and gone. Cinderella was no longer at the ball.

Too bad she couldn't remember how it had ended...or where she was...or how she had gotten there. Even more important, she wished that she hadn't recognized the voice that had spoken in her ear.

Dear God, what have I done?

Emily realized with something very close to shame that she really didn't want to know. What a coward she was.

She continued to lie there, trying to comprehend all that she was discovering. She had no idea how long she lay there, trying to gain enough courage to open her eyes.

Had she managed somehow to go back to the hotel without remembering it? Did it matter, since it was obvious that wherever she was, she wasn't alone.

There was a large, warm hand resting across her rib cage—her bare rib cage—just under her breasts, which were also bare. Even in her painful state, her brain managed to associate the fact that the hand belonged to the same man who had recently spoken to her. Despite its sluggishness and all those jackhammers working away so industriously, her brain also notified her that, considering all of the evidence at hand, she had just spent the night with Jeremy Jones.

Terri had wanted her to get out and enjoy life, but Emily was fairly certain this wasn't what Terri had in mind when she suggested the trip to Las Vegas. What could possibly have come over her to have behaved so out of character? It was one thing to pretend to be Cinderella, to be outgoing and charming and witty, but Cinderella had sense enough to go home alone.

How had she ended up in bed with Jeremy? Just as important, how had she ended up in bed with Jeremy without remembering the circumstances? And how was she ever going to be able to face herself in a mirror again?

Emily moaned softly, but in the quiet of the room it seemed to echo and reecho around the walls.

The bed shifted slightly, and she barely managed to suppress a second moan.

"How are you feeling this morning?"

How could he sound so wide awake, so healthy, so unashamed, so—words failed her. From the slight note of amusement she detected in his voice, Emily knew that she wasn't fooling him in the least by pretending to be dead . . . or even asleep.

"Fine," she mumbled, hoping that lightning would not strike her for lying, as well as for all her other transgressions.

"Then why are you frowning?" he asked, smoothing the skin between her eyebrows with his finger. She could feel the ridges in her forehead.

Forcing herself to relax her facial muscles, she thought about his question for a moment. The time had come to show him that she was in control of herself, that she wasn't embarrassed, that she was, in fact, able to handle the knowledge that she had awakened in bed with a man.

"I always frown first thing in the morning," she offered in way of an explanation. "Part of my exercise program." She was pleased with her calm, matter-of-fact tone of voice.

He made a noise that sounded suspiciously like a chuckle. "I see."

Emily continued to lie there stiffly beside him, praying for inspiration to know how to get herself out of the current situation with the least amount of awkwardness, when he slid his hand from her rib cage up toward her breast.

Her eyes flew open, and Emily stared into Jeremy's dancing black eyes.

"Is it time to begin your eyelid exercises now?" he asked with a hint of a smile playing around his lips.

Everything seemed so much more real with her eyes open. She couldn't take her gaze from his, and her heart seemed to have joined the rat-a-tat rhythm of the jackhammers in her head. "What are you doing here?"

She had meant the question to sound casual, as though it really didn't matter to her, that she had only inquired out of politeness. Instead, her voice broke into an accusing quaver halfway through her question.

"I live here," he explained, his smile growing.

Emily lifted her head from the pillow and stared with dismay. She was in a room that seemed to be made of glass. Three walls were open to the out-of-doors that looked out into a lush garden enclosed by a high wall. An underground sprinkler system was lavishly flinging water over grass, flowering bushes and multihued flower beds.

Unable to face what the morning had revealed to her, Emily let her head fall back onto the pillow and closed her eyes tightly once again.

"An interesting exercise," he observed. "Probably doesn't do much for your heart, though."

"You'd be surprised," she muttered to herself. Her heart was now outdistancing the jackhammers in its mad race to leave her chest.

"How's your head this morning?"

"Very much in evidence," she managed to mutter between clenched teeth. She flinched when she felt his lips brush against her cheek.

"Poor baby," he murmured. "Let me get you some aspirin. That will probably help some."

Emily opened her eyes when she felt the bed move. Jeremy had rolled away from her and was sitting on the side of the bed. Her eyes widened at the view of unadorned flesh, until she realized that he was wearing underwear, if you could call something so small, wearing apparel. She stared with a certain amount of horrified fascination as the man she'd slept with during the preceding night crossed the room with catlike grace.

There was no denying he had a beautiful, well-honed body. The sleek expanse of tanned skin covered a rippling array of taut muscles.

Nothing in Emily's experience had prepared her for this moment. She had moved into the fast lane with a vengeance.

She placed her arm over her eyes and concentrated on clearing her mind of all thoughts. She focused on visualizing a small white cloud in the sky where she could float away, never to be seen or heard from again.

"Here you are."

With a fatalistic calm, Emily lowered her arm and pushed herself up in bed, making sure the sheet continued to cover her bare breasts. Without looking up, she held out her hand.

"I'm afraid you'll need both hands for the aspirin and the glass of water," Jeremy explained. She could hear the amusement in his voice. No doubt he found her embarrassment at the situation humorous.

Emily fought to keep her composure. Still without looking at him, she tucked the sheet under her arms, then slowly raised her head until she could meet his gaze.

The expression of tenderness on his face caught her off guard. She felt a sudden surge of tears and fought to control them. Taking the aspirin and water from him, she swallowed them, trying hard to keep her gaze from wandering over his tanned, well-muscled body.

There ought to be a law to prohibit a man from looking so good. No wonder she hadn't had a chance. With his looks, background and experience he'd known exactly what to do to get her into his bed. Although she wasn't totally without experience, she'd never spent the night with a man, and she'd certainly never considered making love with someone she'd just met.

Quite frankly, she hadn't a clue how to handle it.

Emily watched Jeremy walk across the room and return the glass to the bathroom. Then she silently watched him return to bed and stretch out beside her once more.

"I suppose you're used to this sort of thing," she offered in an attempt to sound casual, wishing he'd crawled under the sheet instead of lying there bare beside her. But then again, if he'd crawled beneath the sheet he would be able to touch her again, and she knew she'd not be able to handle that at the moment.

"As a matter of fact, I'm not. I don't think I've ever before spent a night quite like last night," he said in a whimsical tone of voice.

His comment did nothing to help her state of mind. Granted, she knew next to nothing about lovemaking, but he didn't have to make it quite so clear that she didn't measure up to what he was accustomed to.

Emily wasn't sure which was worse. Making love with a man you didn't know, making love with a man and not remembering it, or making love and finding out you were terrible at it.

With a soft moan, she hid her face in her hands.

"Does your head still hurt?" he asked, his sympathy evident in his soothing tone of voice.

She shook her head.

"Is there anything else the matter?"

She nodded her head.

"Do you want to talk about it?"

She was quiet for a few moments, then slowly dropped her hands into her lap and looked at him with a resigned expression. "I'm sorry."

Jeremy had turned to face her and was propped up on one elbow. He looked puzzled. "About what?"

"Everything. About this—" she waved her hand at the bed "—about not being what you're used to, about—"

"Hey, hey, wait a minute. What do you mean, not being what I'm used to? What gave you the idea I was comparing you with someone?"

"Well, you said you'd not spent a night like this with anyone else."

He began to smile. "And you took that as an insult? I didn't mean it that way, believe me. I enjoyed being with you." He lifted her hand and placed a kiss on the tip of each finger. "Very much. I find you fascinating. You're so different from—"

"You see? You're doing it again."

Jeremy grinned sheepishly. "I'm sorry. It's just that you're so real, somehow. So refreshingly honest. You're fun, and you're intelligent, and you're sexy as hell, and—"

"Oh, Jeremy, you don't have to pretend. I understand that you're trying to be nice about everything, and I appreciate it. I really do. But it isn't necessary."

"I'm not sure what has upset you. I know that you had too much to drink last night and—"

"I what? Don't be silly. I don't drink."

"So you kept insisting last night, right up until the time you passed out in my arms."

"Ooohh." She snatched her fingers from him and slid down into the bed. Staring at the ceiling she asked, "Are you telling me that I was not drinking fruit punch last night?"

"I tried to explain to you last night that those fruit punch drinks were liberally laced with rum."

"Rum." She tasted the word thoughtfully.

"Um-hmm."

"So I was drunk."

"That's one way of expressing it. I would just say that the late night and the unaccustomed liquor all contributed to your getting very tired and deciding to go to sleep. Unfortunately we weren't anywhere near a bed when you made that decision." He was quiet for a moment. "Remember you're still operating on Little Rock time, which is two hours later than here."

She slowly turned her head on the pillow. "You know who I am?" she asked with more than a hint of dismay in her voice. There went her last hope for anonymity.

"Wasn't I supposed to?" he asked, surprised at the question.

"Henry and Cynthia thought I looked so different. None of us thought you'd recognize me."

"Ah, but Cinderella could never disguise those eyes...or that fair complexion...or that wealth of beautiful hair. I'll admit it was quite a metamorphosis from the woman who stepped off the plane. But I had no problem recognizing you, Emily. None in the least."

So her fairy-tale pretense last night was wasted. Even worse, there was no way she could pretend to be someone else now. The ball was definitely over, and Cinderella had turned into a pumpkin.

"I'd like to go back to my hotel," she finally said.

He smoothed her hair away from her face. "There's really no hurry, is there? We have all day before our date tonight."

Their date. She'd forgotten about that. Emily had hoped she could go back to the hotel and never have to see him again. How was it possible to face him after all that had happened? She had had too much to drink, she'd fallen asleep, she'd—

"You might as well know," she began in as firm a voice as possible, "that I am not used to behaving the way I did last night."

"I know," he said soothingly.

"I know you must think I'm brazenly forward—"

"On the contrary, I find your shyness rather captivating, even though it's caused me some very frustrating hours." He grinned as he reached for a curl and began to wind it around his finger.

"The thing is—" She paused, trying to gain some nonexistent courage. "You see, the problem is that...I mean, it's just that—"

He watched her with an interested expression on his face.

"Yes?"

"I don't even remember making love to you!" she finally blurted out.

She felt him tense beside her. His hand dropped away from her hair. She could feel him staring at her. With tremendous effort she forced herself to meet his eyes. And blinked. He looked furious.

"Are you saying that you think we made love last night?" he said in an ominously low voice.

Why should he sound so insulted? And surprised? And angry?

"Didn't we?" she managed to ask.

"Do you think I'm the type of man who would take advantage of a woman who'd obviously had too much to drink?"

"But, but what am I doing here with you? Why else would you be—" She waved her hand helplessly at his unadorned body.

"I brought you in here last night because it was the closest bedroom to the terrace. I could not get you awake. When I realized you were sound asleep I decided to leave you here. I knew you wouldn't be comfortable in that dress so I took it off you, not realizing the only thing you had on beneath it was a handkerchief-size pair of briefs.

She stared at him for a moment in silence. "You mean that nothing happened between us?"

"That's exactly what I mean, and I resent the fact that you think I'd take advantage of a situation like that."

"But you slept with me."

"That's right. And that's all I did—sleep. After all, this is my room. And the bed was certainly big enough for both of us."

"Oh."

"Is that all you can say?"

"What more do you want me to say?" Suddenly she was feeling as though a hundred-pound weight had been lifted from her shoulders.

"I think you owe me an apology."

"An apology?" She stared at him as though he'd begun speaking in a foreign language. "I'm supposed to apologize for not making love to you?" she asked slowly, a tinge of anger echoing in her tones.

"Of course not! You owe me an apology for thinking I'd take advantage of you."

"Oh." She thought about that for a moment. She supposed he was right. Everything had hit her so quickly as soon as she'd awakened, she really hadn't been able to think very clearly. She certainly hadn't had time to think everything through. "I'm sorry," she said gently. "I didn't mean to insult you."

His irritated expression almost caused her to smile as she began to see the humor in the situation. After all, nothing had happened, other than that she had made a complete fool of herself the night before.

She could live with that. From what she could remember of the night before, making a fool of herself was almost worth experiencing the magical time she had spent with Jeremy. Now that she had time to think about it, he'd been nothing like what she'd imagined him to be.

Jeremy had made her feel very special, and she owed him a great deal of appreciation for the way he'd treated her, not only at the party, but by taking care of her last night. Why, he'd even known she would have a headache and had tried to ease her pain.

Emily smiled at him, her good humor restored.

"I don't know why you should jump to such a conclusion in the first place," he said rather grimly.

Emily glanced around the room and back at him. "You have to admit, the situation is open to interpretation."

"And you immediately interpreted it as though I'm a seducer of unconscious women."

She began to laugh. "Yes, I suppose I did. But you really don't need to be so insulted, you know. After all, this situation is a little unusual." She glanced at him from the corner of her eye. "At least for me."

"Well, I don't normally wake up with someone in my bed, either, despite what you may have read in the gossip columns."

Emily sobered at the reminder of who he was and the fact that no matter how innocent the night had been, all the appearances were to the contrary.

"Who knows that I spent the night?" she asked urgently.

"Why? Do you expect to get your name in the papers?"

Emily didn't care for the sarcasm. "I'd prefer not to be mentioned, thank you, anyway."

"No one knows where you slept. And even more importantly, no one really cares. So you can get rid of the frightened-virgin expression on your face."

For the first time since she'd awakened that morning, Emily forgot about herself and her circumstances. She could feel Jeremy's anger and even more important, was aware of the pain that he'd tried to cover with sarcasm.

She turned to him so that they were facing each other. "I'm sorry you were offended, Jeremy. I didn't mean to hurt you in any way." Without thinking, she reached out and stroked his unshaven jaw, enjoying the roughness against her sensitive palm.

Slowly turning his head, he kissed her palm. The anger in his eyes seemed to fade as another light appeared. This one looked even more dangerous to Emily's peace of mind.

He reached over and put his arm around her. Then, leaning forward slightly, he placed his lips on hers. The tender sweetness of his kiss seemed to melt Emily, and her resistance fled as she relaxed and enjoyed his touch.

Jeremy shifted until his leg lay across her, still covered by the sheet. He rested his elbows on either side of her head and began to explore her face with his mouth, placing light butterfly kisses on her nose, across her brow, and, when her eyes drifted closed while she savored the sensations created by his touch, he placed tiny kisses on each eyelid with such a feathery caress that she scarcely felt them.

As he continued to explore, he discovered the vulnerable area of her neck just below her ear and began to concentrate his attention there with kisses and tiny nibbles that caused chills to scatter across her body.

Emily could no longer lie still under his touch. Restlessly turning her head, she found herself staring into Jeremy's eyes only inches away, their passionate heat stirring her even more than his kisses had done.

His kiss this time was no longer light and gentle. He kissed her as though starving for the taste and touch of her, and Emily found herself responding. He'd invaded her mouth with his tongue like a marauding conqueror determined to establish his claim on her.

She found herself with her arms around his neck, her hands playing in his hair, reveling in the marvelous awareness of all her senses— She felt him pressed against her, so that she was aware of his strong, muscular body, obviously affected by her.... She heard his quickened breathing...smelled the provocative scent of his spicy cologne that still lingered...tasted the heat of his mouth as it burned against hers...and when she opened her eyes, she saw the slight sheen of moisture across his brow as he fought to stay in control of his own emotions.

He pulled back from her slightly, his breathing hoarse and ragged. "Emily?"

"Hmm?"

"I want to make love to you."

"I know," she whispered with a smile.

"Is it all right? I mean, are you protected?"

Of course not. Why would she be? Her mind began to realize what was happening and why. She had been put to bed last night because she'd had too much to drink. Now this morning she was ready to—

"No!" she said, suddenly moving away from him.

"Easy, easy," he said smoothly. "There's no problem. I can—"

"No! I mean. I don't want to. I—"

He stared at her, shocked at the obvious lie. She'd been melting in his arms, responding to him so beautifully.

"You don't want to?" he repeated slowly.

Emily fought for air. She felt as though she was drowning in her own emotions. She sat up in bed, taking deep breaths.

"You don't understand," she managed to say between breaths.

"I'll certainly agree to that. I never got the impression I was forcing you."

She couldn't look at him. He had fallen back on his pillow and lay there, staring at her with a puzzled expression on his face.

Drawing her knees up, Emily pressed her forehead against her knees. "It's not that I don't want to," she finally said without looking at him. "It's that I can't. I'm not the kind of person who can make love casually."

"And you think I am?"

She thought about that for a moment. Then she turned her head and met his gaze. "I don't know. That's the whole point. I don't know you. I know about you, of course, but I don't know the man that you are, down inside. Our being together may be something really special to you. I know that my being with you has been something really special to me, Jeremy. And I don't want to spoil it by doing something that I'd be embarrassed and ashamed of later."

"I see," he said after a moment.

"I'm sorry if I led you to think differently."

He laughed, a shaky effort but real, nonetheless. "Forget it. I wasn't thinking at all. Of course this is crazy—for both of us. I don't need any entanglements, especially not at the moment. As for you—"

"Yes. As for me, I'm going back to Little Rock, to take up my life again. We're from two different worlds."

"I know. I never meant this to happen when I brought you in here last night."

"I believe you."

"I'm glad, because right at the moment I'm more ashamed of myself than you could possibly imagine. I realized last night that you are very sheltered, and I was very close to taking advantage of you."

"My inexperience shows, does it?"

"No. Your innocence shows. You're so refreshingly candid. You make no pretense about who you are and what you are." He reached up and touched her back where the sheet had fallen away. "You are beautiful through and through. I would hate myself if I took advantage of you." His hand slid up and down her spine.

"In that case, I suggest you refrain from touching me that way. I think I should return to the hotel, don't you?"

His laugh this time was much more natural. He exaggeratedly pulled his hand away from her as though he'd been scorched. Bounding off the bed, he made a deep bow and said, "Your carriage awaits you, my lady, whenever you wish to leave."

Emily could feel color flood her face. Jeremy was making no effort to hide anything from her, including the fact that he was still very much affected by their lovemaking.

She glanced down at herself. "Where is my dress?" she finally managed to ask.

He walked over to a chair and carefully lifted the garment. Coming to her side of the bed he held it out to her. Knowing she had no choice, Emily eased out of bed and hastily drew the dress on. He reached behind her so that his arms were around her and she was pressed against him. With a smile he fastened the dress.

"Feel better?" he asked.

She nodded. "I'll be right back," she said without looking up at him and disappeared into the bathroom, closing the door behind her.

Jeremy stared at the closed door for several moments without moving, trying to come to terms with what was happening to him.

He'd acted totally out of character last night. He'd had a houseful of people visiting for a party, and he'd ignored them while he spent the evening with a woman who shouldn't have meant anything to him. He hadn't even planned to see her until tonight. Henry had assured him that he and Cynthia would keep her entertained.

He hadn't recognized her at first, even though he hadn't admitted that to her. It wasn't until she turned and looked up at him that he recognized those eyes— those unforgettable, haunting eyes. She'd looked beautiful and self-confident, totally self-assured, until he'd looked into her eyes and seen the uncertainty, the vulnerability lurking there.

Cinderella. Was that how she saw herself? What a shock it must have been for her to wake up and find herself in his bed. It would have been even more of a shock if they had continued to make love. If she hadn't stopped him, he would have, and he knew it.

Why? What was it about Emily Hartman that drew him to her? In the three years since his divorce he'd kept a deliberate distance between himself and the women he met. He wanted no more involvements, not after his relationship with Linda had fallen apart.

He didn't like being vulnerable. He didn't appreciate handing another person a weapon to be used against him. Linda had learned how to use his love for Michelle against him. Michelle was his only weakness. And yet— And yet there was something he felt around Emily that he'd never felt around anyone else. He didn't understand it, and quite frankly, it scared the hell out of him.

He walked over to the closet and found a shirt and clean pair of jeans, then dug around for a pair of sneakers. Though the show had closed last night, he still had to work on the new material for his upcoming recording session—hence all the daily rehearsals on top of the shows—and the musical score. He needed to remember that and not allow himself to become distracted.

Jeremy had long since discovered that music was the only thing that could soothe his mind and calm his soul. His body would have to understand that his hormones didn't rule his life. He'd made that mistake once and had learned a valuable lesson.

So. He would take Emily back to the hotel, spend the day playing golf with his friends, take her out for their official date tonight, and that would be that.

He wouldn't see her again. Funny how the thought of never seeing her again seemed to hit a sore spot somewhere inside him. He'd only known her a couple of days. Granted, he had found out a great deal about her last night, had enjoyed her company tremendously, had enjoyed sleeping with her in his arms last night. His reactions were because of the monastic life he'd been leading lately. Perhaps he should do something about that.

He reminded himself once again that he had too much on his mind to spend time thinking about her or anyone else. Jeremy settled down in the chair in front of the glass wall overlooking the garden and waited for Emily to reappear.

His life was complicated enough. No matter how much he was attracted to her, he wasn't going to allow himself to pursue the attraction.

All his resolutions seemed to fly out of his head when she walked out of the bathroom.

She had washed her face and combed her hair. Even without makeup she looked wonderful in the morning light. Her hair fell like a midnight waterfall around her face and over her shoulders.

"Ready to go?" he asked, coming to his feet.

She hadn't seen him when she had first walked into the room, and she glanced around, startled. She looked very shy and unsure of herself now. "There's no reason for you to have to take me back. I can take a cab."

He grinned. "But don't you know? It's common courtesy to return the woman home the next morning after I've slept with her. It would be a serious breach of etiquette to send you back by yourself in a cab."

Jeremy enjoyed watching the color on her face deepen. He discovered that he couldn't keep his eyes off the way the dress fit her. He no longer needed to use his imagination regarding how she looked underneath the shiny material. He could remember each peak and hollow. His fingers itched with the knowledge of how well her breast would fit in the palm of his hand.

He watched as she found her shoes and slipped them on. Then he walked over to the bedroom door. "Would you like some coffee or something before you go?"

"No, thank you," she said in a politely formal voice.

He found himself grinning as he followed her down the hallway.

Why did he feel that he was fighting a losing battle where she was concerned? Not only was she beautiful and intelligent, but she had an adorable personality. She would be so easy to love. Too easy.

Five

Dear Terri,
I'm having a terrific time in Las Vegas. I've been treated like a celebrity. Jeremy Jones is even more wonderful in person than anyone could possibly imagine. He's warm and witty, and makes my knees buckle whenever he kisses me—

Emily paused with a frown. Now why had she put that? She hadn't meant to. Irritated, she wadded up the hotel stationery that she had been writing on and began again.

Dear Terri,
You were right about Las Vegas. I'm so glad I came. Wish you were here.

No. Too trite. Everyone said that sort of thing. She wadded up another page.

Dear Terri,
You were absolutely right. This was just the sort of vacation I needed. I've learned a great deal about myself since I've been here. You wouldn't believe how well I've been treated. And the hotel room looks like something from a fancy movie set.

As for Jeremy, what can I say? He's every woman's dream come true. So you can imagine how I felt when I woke up with him this morning and—

This time she ripped the stationery into shreds and gave up her effort to write. What difference did it make anyway? She'd be home before the letter got there.

She paced over to the window and stared out at another golf course. Las Vegas seemed to be made up of golf courses. She was amazed at the contrast between the deep green of the watered areas and the desolate dryness of the desert around them. Emily was used to the variegated greens of Arkansas. The desert seemed so stark.

Jeremy had been quiet while driving her back to her hotel. Emily hadn't been able to think of anything to say, either. She felt silly dressed so formally while he was in jeans and sneakers, but when he walked her through the lobby to the elevators, no one had given them a second glance.

"You don't have to see me to my room. I'll be fine."

He nodded his head. "I'll pick you up at eight. We have reservations at State Street."

"What is that?"

"It's a restaurant here in town. I think you'll enjoy the food there, as well as the entertainment."

He waited until she was on the elevator before walking away.

Emily knew that something had happened between her and Jeremy that neither one was ready to acknowledge. She was glad to have some time to herself, to try to come to grips with the emotions she'd been experiencing since she'd first met him.

Of course he was unusual—she had known that before she ever met him, but even so, Emily knew he was different from most entertainers. He had allowed her to see a more tender side of him. By looking after her the night before, taking care of her, even protecting her, Jeremy had shown a rare gentleness that she wouldn't have expected to find in any man, much less one who spent so much of his time in the limelight.

She shivered at the memory of the look in his eyes when he'd left her in the lobby. He made no effort to hide the attraction he felt for her. Emily knew that her reaction to him was just as strong.

How did that happen? What was the chemistry between two people that created sparks immediately upon meeting? She hadn't been surprised at her own reaction. But what was happening where he was concerned? How many men would have accepted the sudden halt to their lovemaking without becoming resentful or perhaps even angry?

She turned away from the window. This was no way to be spending her time in Las Vegas. Terri would be sure to ask if she had played the slot machines. Finding her purse, Emily decided to go downstairs for a while and mingle with the people who were there enjoying themselves. For a while she would be a typical tourist, playing the machines and taking in the sights.

Perhaps it would take her mind off the coming evening when once again she and Jeremy would be together.

Jeremy felt as though he'd wasted his day. He'd kept a date with friends on the golf course and was ribbed about his inability to keep his mind on the game. Not that he blamed them. He'd played a lousy round, and he knew it. He also knew why.

He couldn't keep his mind off Emily and the way she had looked, both at the party, then later in his bed. He'd awakened once in the night and discovered that she was using his chest as a pillow. Her hair was draped around him as though it were a shawl cast over his shoulders.

She'd been curled up as though it was the most natural thing in the world for them to be together like that. Jeremy knew that he'd never before experienced the amused frustration that her being in bed with him had caused.

He'd known better than to continue to lie there like that and had eased away from her. He'd gotten up and gone outside into the garden, had watched the moon as it disappeared into the western horizon, and had watched the stars slowly wink out as the light in the east signaled the approach of dawn.

Eventually he'd gone back to bed and to sleep, but even in his sleep he'd been aware of her. She had haunted his dreams, tantalized him with her soft scent and the sound of her gentle breathing.

Now he had to spend another evening with her and pretend that it was all a publicity promotion and that she meant nothing more to him than any other fan who might have won the trip.

Jeremy had never considered himself much of an actor. He wondered if he could get through the evening without telling her what an impact she had made on his life.

More importantly, he wondered what the hell he could do about it. The timing was all wrong, as well as the distance involved.

And did it matter what he felt, anyway? She'd made it clear she wouldn't become involved in a casual relationship with him. He was very much afraid that what he was feeling was too strong to be satisfied with a casual fling, and it scared the hell out of him.

Hours later, Emily looked around the restaurant with interest, trying to keep her gaze away from Jeremy. She had felt a nervous energy emanating from him as soon as she had opened the door.

Their conversation thus far had been light and casual. She'd shared with him the fact that she had won twenty-five dollars in quarters and had bought a souvenir for her niece, and he had described his less-than-spectacular golf game.

But all the while the conversation was taking place, the undercurrents were there between them, too strong to be ignored.

They were seated in a booth with a flickering candle that seemed to cast a sense of intimacy between them. Emily tried to concentrate on the atmosphere instead of the man seated across from her. She gazed pointedly at the pictures of famous people on the walls rather than concentrate on him.

Later while they were studying the menu, Jeremy introduced her to the owner, who had paused by their table to say hello. After he had chatted for a few moments and walked away, Emily noticed there was a framed picture of him and Jeremy hanging nearby.

After they ordered, Jeremy leaned back in the booth and studied her as though he were an artist preparing to paint a portrait. "Is there something wrong?" he asked finally, when she continued to look around the room rather than meet his gaze.

Forcing herself to look at him, she said, "Why do you ask?"

"You've been so quiet since we arrived."

"That's because I gave you my entire history last night," she said with a slight smile. "I thought I'd give you a rest."

"I enjoyed last night," he said quietly. "It's been a long time since anyone was as completely natural with me as you were."

"I'm not usually one to talk much. It must have been the unaccustomed alcohol."

"Last night must have been a series of firsts for you, then," he said with a hint of a grin.

"A gentleman would never have pointed that out," she responded, knowing her cheeks must be glowing in the dark.

"Whatever gave you the impression that I'm a gentleman? Still wrapped up in your fairy tales, by chance?"

She glanced down at her hands, which were clasped in front of her, then slowly up at him. His eyes glowed in the candlelight, and once again she wished he wasn't so attractive. "No. I've put away all my fairy tales and illusions. They can be dangerous."

"Jeremy?"

They glanced up at the owner, who had appeared at the table once again.

"Yes, Frank?"

"Henry's on the phone. Said he needed to speak with you."

Jeremy glanced at Emily, obviously puzzled. Nodding to Frank, he excused himself and left the table.

Within minutes he'd returned. She saw no expression on his face until she looked into his eyes. Then she realized he was upset.

"I'm sorry, Emily. I'm afraid we aren't going to be able to stay for dinner. Something's come up."

Emily hastily slid from the booth. "That's all right. I understand."

They were out in his small sports car in minutes. She watched as he placed the key into the ignition and noticed that his hand was shaking.

"Is it something you can talk about?" she asked quietly.

He glanced at her, then clenched the steering wheel tightly for a moment, before releasing it and starting the engine.

"It seems my ex-wife has had a sudden and totally unexpected change of heart. After I've been trying for months to get custody of my daughter, without success, she's put her on a plane to me."

Emily stared at him in confusion. "You mean now?"

"Yeah. She just called the house a few minutes ago to let me know that Michelle will be arriving at the airport in—" he paused and looked at his watch, then muttered a curse "—less than twenty minutes. It seems she waited until she got home from the airport to call and let anyone know."

"And your daughter's flying alone? Isn't she only—"

"She's five. And yes. Linda put her on the plane alone, at night, without giving anyone any warning."

The car shot around the corner and headed toward the airport.

Emily didn't know what to say. She felt as though he'd forgotten she was in the car until he said, "I'm sorry you had to get involved in this. I would have dropped you off at the hotel, but I don't want to take a chance on Michelle arriving before I can get there. She doesn't need that on top of everything else."

"I don't mind, Jeremy."

"I knew that Linda was being totally irresponsible lately, but this really does it. If I weren't so damned mad at her at the moment, I'd call her and thank her for finally letting go of Michelle. She's put her through all kinds of trauma in the past two years."

"I see."

"I doubt it. Linda has some serious problems, but until she admits she needs help, no one can do anything for her." After a few moments of silence, he said, "What I hate the most is how it's affected Michelle. Linda seems to have done whatever she could to cause Michelle to be afraid of me."

"Oh, no. Surely she wouldn't do that to a child?"

"To be honest, I was shocked at the change in her, myself. The woman I first knew and married would have never behaved this way."

"But couldn't the courts do something?"

"Believe me, I've been pushing them for all I'm worth. But the court system is bogged down with cases, and the social worker said she'd never seen any sign of abuse or neglect."

"Then maybe it wasn't as bad as you thought."

"God, I hope not. Michelle doesn't deserve being treated like a Ping-Pong ball."

They drove the rest of the way in silence. Emily hurried along beside him as he rapidly strode down the concourse to the appropriate gate for the flight from Los Angeles. At least Michelle hadn't been on a long flight. Perhaps she wouldn't be too frightened.

Emily could feel Jeremy's tension mount when the flight was announced. He stood stiffly at the end of the aisle that led from the jetway into the concourse. The doors opened, and an attendant came through, leading a little girl.

Her hair was long, straight and a golden-blond color. She wore a bright red dress with white ruffles on the collar, sleeves and hem. She had on black patent leather shoes that buckled, and she carried a very battered, but obviously well-loved, stuffed rabbit that had one long ear hanging limply over a button eye.

When Emily looked into the large, wary black eyes that stared back from a face too solemn for a five-year-old child, she lost her heart.

Jeremy went down on one knee and held out his arms. "Hello, Michelle, love. Welcome home."

Michelle seemed to freeze like a frightened animal as soon as she spotted Jeremy. She hung behind the attendant who was trying to coax her forward.

"There's your daddy, Michelle," the attendant said with a smile. "Did you know you had a famous daddy?" The woman glanced at Jeremy. "I don't need to ask for identification, do I, Mr. Jones? Michelle looks just like you."

The smile he gave her was distracted and without much humor. His eyes never left Michelle's face. "Do you remember me, honey?" he asked, his anxious tone tearing at Emily.

Michelle let go of the attendant's hand in order to get a better grip on her rabbit. She wrapped both arms firmly around it in a stranglehold. She stared at Jeremy for what seemed like hours without saying anything. Finally she nodded uncertainly.

"I have your room all ready for you and Robby. And Uncle Henry is waiting to see you. Do you remember Uncle Henry? And Cynthia?"

Michelle dropped her eyes and stared at her toes without responding.

The flight attendant stroked Michelle's head gently. "I enjoyed having you with us on this flight, Michelle. I have to go back now, okay?"

Michelle glanced up at the woman. Large tears welled up in Michelle's eyes and ran down her cheeks, but she didn't say a word.

Emily couldn't remember a time when she'd felt so helpless. She could see that Michelle's tears had unnerved Jeremy. He had frozen in the same position, his arms reaching for Michelle. Later, she didn't know what possessed her to intrude where she had no business, but she found herself walking over to Michelle, smiling and holding out her hand.

"Hi, Michelle. My name's Emily. I used to have a rabbit like Robby once. Only I called mine Peter Cottontail."

Michelle looked up at her, her eyes so much like Jeremy's it was like seeing him all over again. "That's a funny name, Peter Cottontail," she said softly.

Emily laughed. "I know. I like Robby better. Did you name him that?"

Michelle shook her head. "My daddy named him."

"Oh, I see." So Jeremy had named her rabbit . . . the rabbit that appeared to be her most prized possession. Did he understand the significance of that? She hoped so. "How would you like to take a ride in your daddy's car? It's a little bitty one. I bet I'll have to sit on your lap, it's so small."

Michelle looked her up and down. "You're too big. You'd smash me."

"I hadn't thought about that. Maybe you'd better sit on my lap, what do you think?"

Michelle looked over at Jeremy, who was watching intently from the sidelines. Then she looked back at Emily. "Are you my daddy's mommy?" she asked.

Oh, dear God, Emily thought, closing her eyes in a quick prayer. What now?

Jeremy stood and took the necessary steps to where Michelle waited. Swinging her up in his arms, he said, "No, love. This is Emily, a friend of mine."

Michelle's solemn expression didn't change. "Mommy said she wasn't going to be my mommy anymore. She said she was sick, and she was going away."

Jeremy hugged her close, and Emily watched as he tried to get a grip on his emotions. "She was only teasing, Michelle. Your mother won't go away and leave you."

"She already did," came the muffled response. She pushed back from Jeremy. "She took me to the airplane and said I had to stay until the plane left. And then she went away."

What sort of woman would say and do such things to an innocent child? Emily wondered. Were there really such uncaring, unthinking people in the world who would needlessly upset a child with such selfish actions and comments?

As they walked through the concourse to the parking garage, Emily chatted with Michelle much like she talked with Patti, her niece. She was thankful that she'd had some experience around children, even though she'd had very little contact with a child who had been treated as Michelle had obviously been.

By the time they reached the car, Michelle was responding to Emily, telling her about Robby and about Matilda, a rag doll that was in the suitcase they had claimed at the baggage area.

She willingly settled herself into Emily's lap.

What a love she is, Emily thought, holding the little girl close. She was surprised at how Michelle had responded to her under the circumstances. She still seemed withdrawn from Jeremy.

"Would you mind if I took her on home now?" he asked quietly when he got into the car beside them.

Emily smiled. "Not at all."

"This wasn't exactly what we had in mind for you, for your date with Jeremy Jones."

"I don't mind."

"We'll plan it again in another day or so."

"Oh, no. It really doesn't matter. I need to—"

"It does matter. To me. So humor me a little, okay?"

She glanced around, surprised at the drawn look around his eyes and the firmness of his chin. He talked as though their time together was important to him, and Emily discovered that she didn't want to argue with him. For whatever reason, she knew that any time spent in Jeremy's presence would have a special significance to her.

Michelle rested her head on Emily's breast. "Are you sleepy?" Emily asked softly.

Michelle nodded her head.

Emily laid her hand against Michelle's silky hair, stroking it softly, loving the feel of it. When they reached his home, she waited for Jeremy to take Michelle out of her arms before she moved.

Michelle raised her head sleepily from his shoulder and looked at Emily. "Are you going to sleep with me?"

Emily smiled. "No. I don't live here."

"Don't leave," Michelle whispered, clutching her rabbit. "Please don't leave me."

Emily realized that Michelle either wasn't used to men, or was shy with Jeremy. She had been comfortable with the flight attendant, even crying when she'd had to leave her. Now she was already reaching out to Emily, someone she'd known less than an hour.

Emily glanced helplessly up at Jeremy.

"There are twin beds in Michelle's room, Emily, if you'd like to stay. But that's up to you. None of this is your problem."

They had entered the house, and Henry was waiting for them.

"There's my girl! Come here to Uncle Henry, darlin'."

Michelle took a tighter grip on Jeremy's neck and buried her head.

Henry looked nonplussed. "Doesn't she remember me?"

"She's just tired, Henry," Jeremy explained. "I think we all are. I'm going to see about getting her into bed."

He started down the hallway. Emily watched uncertainly, not knowing what to do. Henry waved her into one of the rooms off the wide hallway. "Can I get you something to drink?"

The idea had considerable merit. "Yes, if you have something cool and nonalcoholic."

He walked over to a bar in the corner. "We have everything. What would you like?"

Emily named a soft drink, which he opened and poured over ice and brought to her. She sipped it gratefully.

"How was dinner?"

"I'm afraid we didn't make it that far before you called."

"Then we'd better see about getting you something to eat."

"No, that's all right. I'm really not hungry." She studied her drink for a few moments in silence. "Jeremy seems to be taking Michelle's arrival hard."

"I'm not surprised, although having her here is a real stroke of luck. Knowing Jeremy, he's just upset at the way Linda has handled everything. Tonight was no exception. There was no reason for her not to have given him some sort of warning of her intentions. The woman's got some real problems."

"He seems to love her very much."

"Who, Linda? Not on your life. She's put him through hell."

"I was thinking about Michelle."

"Oh. Well, yeah. He's always been absolutely silly about her. Used to spend every spare minute of his time with her, which used to irritate Linda. I think Linda was actually jealous of her own daughter. Of course Linda used to be jealous over anything and everything about Jeremy. She wanted to possess him so totally he felt her stranglehold even when she wasn't around." Henry shook his head. "Jeremy tried to help her, tried to get counseling for her. For a while after the divorce, she seemed to come out of it, made a home for Michelle, allowed Jeremy visitation rights."

He walked over to the window and stared out into the night. "Then a couple of years ago she started acting really strange—refused to allow him to see Michelle. When he would call, Michelle wouldn't talk with him. Linda insisted Michelle didn't want him around her."

"How sad."

"Yes. Linda spread her pain to everyone around her. Unfortunately Jeremy and Michelle suffered as much as Linda, and they were helpless to make any changes." He glanced around. "I'm not sure why I'm telling you all of this."

"Don't worry. I appreciate the confidence, and I won't repeat it."

He walked over and sat down across from her. "You know, I've never seen Jeremy the way he was last night."

"What do you mean?"

"He seemed to be enjoying you so much. Until I heard him laugh at something you had shared with him, I hadn't realized how long it had been since I'd heard him laugh, seen him relaxed and enjoying himself." Henry took a sip of his drink. "You've been good for him."

"I'm glad. I like him very much. He's quite a man."

"Yes, he is. He's been hurt very badly, and he's learned not to get close to very many people. But for some reason he's allowed you to get close to him."

She remembered waking up with him in bed and knew that her face had turned a fiery red. Just as she was hoping that Henry hadn't noticed, he said, "My, whatever did I say to cause such a reaction?"

"Nothing, really."

"Is it possible that Jeremy's already shared how he feels about you?"

She shook her head.

He laughed. "Well, if his golf game today was any indication, his mind has certainly been somewhere else." He smiled as he watched her twist her glass in her fingers. "I'm sorry. I didn't mean to embarrass you. I just wanted you to know that it's obvious to anyone who knows Jeremy that you have made quite an impression on him. I didn't want you returning to Little Rock thinking that he would have treated anyone who had come out here the way he has you."

"Thank you for sharing that with me."

"Emily?"

Both she and Henry turned around at the sound of Jeremy's voice. He looked and sounded distraught. "I'm sorry to bother you, but she doesn't want me to undress her, or help her in any way. I don't want to upset her any more than necessary. Would you mind supervising her, making sure she's all right?"

Emily set her glass down and stood. "I'd be happy to help, Jeremy. Just show me where she is."

"She's next door to my bedroom, and you know—" He paused and glanced at Henry. "I'll show you where," he said, stepping back from the doorway when she joined him.

They walked down the long hallway, and she paused at the door that he indicated and glanced around at him. "Trying to protect my good name?" she asked with a smile.

He wore an odd expression on his face. "I suppose I was. It's no one's business where you spent last night."

"At this rate, you could have saved yourself a great deal of trouble by not booking me at the hotel."

"What do you mean?"

"There's no reason for me to go back there tonight. I'll be glad to stay here and keep Michelle company her first night. I'm sure she'll grow used to you again quickly enough, but I don't mind easing the transition for her."

They were standing close together in the dimly lit hallway, speaking in low tones.

"I'm really sorry about this," he said.

"I'm not. I'm honored that I had the opportunity to meet your daughter, Jeremy. You have every right to be very proud of her."

"So much for your romantic evening with Jeremy Jones."

"You would have had a heck of a time improving on last night's romantic evening, you know."

He slowly pulled her to him, so that she was leaning against him. "I would very much like to improve on that evening. The next time I have you in my bed, I'll guarantee that you won't sleep through it."

She went up on tiptoe and kissed him gently on the lips. "There won't be a next time, Jeremy. The ball is over, and it's time for Cinderella to go home."

The kiss he gave her was anything but gentle. It was filled with his need for her, not a sexual need, but a need to share with someone what he was feeling at the moment.

He was scared—scared that Michelle would continue to be frightened of him, scared that he wouldn't be able to be all that she needed in a parent, scared that he would prove to be inadequate.

Without words, Emily tried to reassure him with her presence, with her response, with her love. When she finally pulled away from him, she was glad that it was too dark for him to see the tears that had filled her eyes.

"I'll see you in the morning, Jeremy. Don't worry. Everything's going to work out all right. Just wait and see."

She opened the door and peeked in. Michelle was sitting up in bed in her nightgown, clutching her rabbit. "Are you going to sleep with me tonight?"

"If you'd like me to."

"That would be nice," Michelle said politely.

Emily looked over at Jeremy, who still stood in the doorway. "How about giving your daddy a good-night kiss?"

Michelle studied the tall man for a moment, then held out her arms. He slowly walked in and sat down beside her. Giving her a kiss and hug, he said, "Good night, punkin."

Michelle almost smiled, but not quite. "I'm not a punkin."

"Oh, pardon me. I must have you confused with someone else," he explained in a serious tone of voice.

He got up and started toward the door.

"Daddy?"

He turned around.

"You forgot to kiss her—" she pointed to Emily "—good-night."

"Her name is Emily," he said, hesitantly approaching Emily.

Emily kissed him on the cheek. "Good night, Jeremy. I hope you sleep well."

"I doubt that I'll do much sleeping with all that's happened." He glanced over at Michelle. "I still can't believe she's here."

"She'll be okay. Give her a day or two."

They'd kept their voices low. When they turned to look at Michelle, they found her cuddled into bed, still clutching her bedraggled rabbit.

Jeremy grinned. "I'm sorry I don't have anyone for you to cuddle up with for the night."

"Don't worry about it. I'm used to sleeping alone."

"So am I. But it was rather nice to wake up and find you in my bed, at that."

"I think we can put last night out of our minds, now, don't you?"

"Maybe you can. I may have some difficulty." Leaning over, he gave her a hard, brief kiss, then walked out of the room without looking back.

Emily undressed slowly. After taking a quick shower in the adjoining bathroom, she came back out into the room, wearing her slip. Tiptoeing over to Michelle, she adjusted the covers.

"Good night, Emily," Michelle whispered.

"Good night, sweetheart," Emily replied, a lump forming in her throat.

It really wasn't fair at all. First the father, then the daughter, had managed to steal her heart without trying.

Terri had been right. After her trip to Las Vegas, nothing would ever be the same for Emily.

She'd been shaken out of her cocoon and discovered that the whole wide world was out there. Never had she felt so vulnerable, but she wouldn't have missed the experience for anything.

Six

The first thing Emily saw when she opened her eyes the next morning was a solemn pair of black eyes not more than six inches away, staring at her from beneath a fringe of golden-blond hair.

This is getting to be a habit, she thought with a sigh, *waking up to find myself in bed with someone.*

"Did I wake you up?" Michelle whispered.

"No."

"I'm glad. Mama said I was never s'posed to wake her up."

"Have you been awake long?"

Michelle shrugged her shoulders.

"Can you tell time?"

"Sometimes."

"Only sometimes?"

"Well, sometimes there's numbers, and I know my numbers, but sometimes the hands are pointing to different numbers, and I don't know what they mean."

"Oh, I see. So you can read a digital clock, but not a regular one?"

"I guess so," Michelle agreed without much interest. "You wanna meet Matilda?"

Emily smiled. That was the most enthusiasm she had heard from Michelle since they had met.

"I would be delighted to meet Matilda."

She watched as Michelle slid off the mattress and went over to her bed. Picking up a floppy rag doll with multicolored hair, she returned and crawled up next to Emily.

Matilda wore a silver lamé jumpsuit, high heels, assorted bracelets and necklaces, and her face was heavily painted. "This is Matilda?" Emily asked, trying not to react negatively to something Michelle obviously admired.

Michelle giggled. "Uh-huh. Miz Rodriguez, who used to come stay with me a lot, made her for me. She calls her a punk rocker."

Emily could not prevent a laugh from escaping her. "Mrs. Rodriguez is quite talented, isn't she?"

"Uh-huh. Is she going to come stay with me here?"

"I have no idea, darling. Would you like her to?"

"I don't like to stay by myself. I get scared."

"Of course you do. You won't have to stay by yourself with your daddy. Is that what you thought?"

Michelle studied her gravely for several moments in silence. "Mama used to leave me by myself, but then

I cried and cried when she'd get ready to go, and she finally got Miz Rodriguez to visit me when she left."

"I see." Was this what had caused Jeremy to try to get custody? What a nightmare that must have been for him. No wonder everyone was relieved to have Michelle here now.

There was a tap on the door, and Michelle scrambled off the bed to answer it.

"Good morning, ladies," Jeremy said when the door opened. Emily thought he seemed relaxed and happy, lounging in the doorway, until she looked closely into his eyes. The strain still showed there. "I thought I heard some giggling and laughing going on in here, and I didn't want to miss any of the fun." His gaze zeroed in on Emily, who had hastily rearranged the covers. "Did you sleep all right?"

Emily nodded. Michelle threw her arms around Jeremy's waist and looked up at him with a big smile. "Am I really going to live here with you, Daddy?"

Jeremy picked her up and sat down on the end of her bed, setting her on his lap. "You bet you are. I've missed you so much. I begged and begged your mama to let you come and stay with me. She finally felt sorry for me, so she said okay. But we'll go see her whenever you want to."

"Mama's sick."

"I know, darlin'. But she's going to get better." He glanced at Emily. "So what would you ladies like to do today?"

Emily smiled. "I'm going to go back to the hotel and pack. There's probably a flight I can get out of here today if I check."

"You can't do that. I've already made reservations for our dinner date." He looked down at Michelle. "Cynthia and Uncle Henry want to come over and watch a Disney movie with you this evening—maybe pop some corn. Would you like that?"

"What movie?" Michelle, ever the pragmatic one, asked.

"I don't know. Perhaps you and Cynthia could discuss that."

"Really, Jeremy, there's no reason for you to leave her. I've had a wonderful time. I don't need another evening."

Jeremy's black-eyed gaze pinned her where she sat, propped up against the bed. "But what about my needs, Emily? Have you ever considered that I might need an evening with you before you walk out of my life? One evening that isn't interrupted in some fashion?"

Michelle looked from one adult to the other, then leaned back against her father with a sigh of contentment. Emily almost smiled. Thank God children could generally make rapid adjustments to a changing environment. How frightening it must be for them to be without any control or power over their most basic needs. Emily felt blessed that she'd been raised in a stable environment, even if it had been more public than she would have wished. Compared to what Michelle had already faced in her life, Emily's fears had been small, indeed.

Her gaze went back to Jeremy. Two pairs of identical black eyes watched her carefully. She shrugged.

"All right. I'll stay. But I absolutely have to go home tomorrow."

Jeremy nodded. "Thank you."

Hours later those words continued to ring through her mind. . . .

Emily lay in the large tub that took up a goodly portion of the bathroom in her suite of rooms at the hotel, reviewing the past several hours.

Jeremy and Michelle had convinced her to spend the day with them, giving her only enough time to return to the hotel and find something more casual to wear, because most of their day was spent outdoors.

Emily hadn't really expected to wear the sleeveless blouse and slacks anywhere, but had packed them to have something to lounge in while she was resting in her room.

Obviously Jeremy didn't intend for her to spend much time in her room.

So Emily was given a firsthand view of Jeremy with his daughter. More than once she wondered how many people had seen this private side of Jeremy and how strange were the circumstances that had given her the opportunity.

She watched them feeding the ducks at one of the city parks and listened to Michelle's squeals when the ducks came up close to her. Emily watched as Michelle grew more comfortable around her father, talking to him more, touching him with a shy hand, smiling up at him with an adorable grin.

And Jeremy. . . Never had Emily seen such a tender expression on anyone's face. His continued patience with Michelle touched Emily. He acted very natural with her, as though being with a five-year-old child made him comfortable and relaxed. He seemed to have all the time in the world for her, although he made sure that Emily was included in everything they were doing.

Meeting both father and daughter had been an experience she knew that she would never forget.

Stirring in the warm water of her bath, Emily reminded herself that it was time to go home, time to pick up the threads of her real life and forget her fantasy world.

She had one more night with him. A night he had given to her that was not part of the promotion, despite what he said. Emily discovered that she wanted this night with him very much.

For the past several hours, Emily had come face-to-face with her emotions. Although she was twenty-nine years old, she had never allowed herself to open up to a man. She'd never allowed herself to be close to any but a select group within her family circle, where she'd felt safe.

Instead of playing the role of Cinderella, she felt more as though she'd played the role of Sleeping Beauty until Jeremy had come into her life.

Now she was awake, and it frightened her.

Why couldn't he have been an insurance salesman or someone local, so that the possibility of a relationship wouldn't be ludicrous?

Emily had spent most of her adult years without a man in her life. It was likely that her life would continue in a similar pattern. She would probably end up, as Terri had threatened, like Aunt Tabitha.

So why was she mooning over someone as unattainable as Jeremy Jones?

Sitting up suddenly in the cooling water, Emily knew she'd been daydreaming long enough. Climbing out, she quickly dried herself and went into the other room to dress. She had decided to wear the cream-colored suit she had worn on the plane, this time with a raspberry-colored blouse that gave her face a hint of color. She wanted to remind both of them of the woman she was, not the woman she'd been while there in Las Vegas.

Brushing out her hair, she frowned for a moment. The salon had not shortened her hair, but they had trimmed and layered it, so that it was much shorter around her face, framing it. Now she couldn't pull it back into its customary style.

Instead, her hair continued to fall into soft waves that seemed to emphasize the line of her jaw, the slight hollow of her cheeks and her wide-set eyes.

She heard a knock on the door in the other room, and Emily ran into the bedroom and grabbed her shoes, hastily shoving her toes into them. Trying to breathe calmly, she forced herself to walk across the room and open the door.

Jeremy wore a suede jacket the color of butter, with chocolate-brown slacks. He looked sensational, as always.

His smile widened when he saw her. "No Cinderella tonight? It's back to the convent, is it?"

She stepped back. "No. It's more like going back to being me. Come in."

When she closed the door, he took her hand. "I'm sorry. I didn't mean that as a put-down. You have to admit there's quite a difference between this demure suit and the two gowns that you've worn before."

She couldn't resist touching his clean-shaven cheek with her fingertips. "I know. And I wanted you to see who I really am. All of this has been wonderfully fun and exciting, but deep down I'm still Emily Hartman from Little Rock, Arkansas, who works in the accounting department and once had a date with the very famous Jeremy Jones." Leaning up and kissing him softly on the cheek, she said, "And believe me, she'll never forget it."

If only his eyes weren't so expressive. A flash of light seemed to flare up with her words. Then, as though keeping himself under careful control, the light dimmed and became a subdued glow.

Emily didn't know where they went, what they ordered or what the food tasted like. She let herself go, drifting along on a sea of sensation, enjoying the present, knowing that she was storing memories of their time together.

At one point she groped for a safe subject. "How was Michelle when you left?"

"Tired. She'd had her dinner and was halfway through a movie with Cynthia. It's my guess she was asleep before it was over."

"She's very lovable."

"I think so, but then, she would be to me."

"I know you're pleased to have her here."

"Relieved is a better word. I've been trying to convince Linda for months to get some help. She must have realized that she couldn't continue to place Michelle in such an unhappy environment.''

Emily was thankful that Henry had shared some of the history between them because she didn't want Jeremy to be reminded of the situation by discussing it. It was almost as though she could feel his pain.

"She'll be starting school this fall, won't she?"

"Yes."

"Do you live here year round?"

"No. This is the time we generally go on tour, but I decided against it this year. We didn't get the release out in time, which is the purpose of our tours—to promote. And I'm working on the musical score of a movie."

"That's quite a departure for you, isn't it?"

"Yes, but one I'm enjoying."

Once again Emily felt the two levels of communication going on between them. He was showing her in every glance, touch and inflection that he wanted her, that he needed her, that he would miss her once she was out of his life.

Jeremy rarely took his eyes off her. The table they shared was small, and his knees unobtrusively brushed against hers as though the touch was accidental, until she realized there was a gentle rhythm to his touch.

He kept reaching out so that his hand touched hers, then he would gently stroke its length from wrist to fingertip. Everywhere he touched caused a tingle within her.

And his eyes. His beautiful, expressive eyes seemed to speak in a language so sensuous, so filled with feeling that Emily felt hypnotized by them.

And then it was time to leave.

He escorted her back to her suite without speaking.

"Would you like to come in?" she asked when he handed her the key after opening her door.

He looked at her in silence, then nodded, and Emily knew that her invitation had told him without words that she was not willing to allow the evening to end without once more holding him in her arms.

"Would you like something to drink?" she asked a little nervously once they were inside. "The bar is very well stocked."

"Emily—"

She turned back to him. "Yes?"

"You don't have to be nervous. I have no intention of taking advantage of you."

She clasped her fingers together. "I know that, Jeremy."

"Then why are you so edgy?"

Emily tried to smile. "I don't know. I guess it's because I don't want you to go just yet, and I don't know what to say to—"

He smiled and took her hand. Leading her to the sofa he motioned for her to sit. He sat down beside her and placed his arm along the back of the seat behind her head.

"All you had to do was ask. Michelle is no doubt sound asleep, but even if she awakens, Henry and Cynthia are both there."

"I know you're busy—"

"I don't want this evening to end, either, you know," he said softly. He leaned over and kissed her gently on the lips.

"I hate goodbyes," she admitted breathlessly after a moment.

"It doesn't have to be," Jeremy said carefully.

"What do you mean?"

"My schedule's flexible enough that I could work out ways to visit you."

"And you would do that?"

"I can't think of anything that would give me more pleasure."

She smiled and laid her head on his shoulder. "I can't believe this."

"Believe it."

Tilting her head back to look at him, she said, "We hardly know each other."

"In many ways I feel as though I've known you all my life."

"I know the feeling. I have to keep reminding myself that you are Jeremy Jones and not—" She paused and glanced at him speculatively. "Have you ever considered selling insurance?"

He looked at her in surprise. "What are you talking about?"

"Oh, nothing. Just wishful thinking, I suppose."

"You mean you'd prefer that I sell insurance to singing for a living?" When she didn't answer, he nudged her. "Why?"

"Because your life is so public. It's based on being well-known and I—"

"Yes?"

"I suppose I've always been such a private person that the thought of your life-style frightens me."

"But it's my life-style that enables me to do what I want to do. And that's very important to me."

"I know."

"But you're very important to me, too. If it will make it any easier on you, I'll promise to wear disguises when I come to see you."

She laughed. "Great idea. Why didn't I think of that?"

"I don't ever want you to be ashamed of being seen with me," he said quietly.

"It isn't that. It's the lack of privacy, as though the world has a right to know who you're seeing, and why. And the speculation. Don't you ever get tired of it?"

"I don't give it a thought. I live my life the way I want to live it, and I don't care what others think. I'm hoping that eventually you'll feel the same way."

"I'll try."

He stood up. "For now, I'm going so that you can get some sleep."

She nodded, already feeling the lump forming in her throat. She knew what he'd just told her. He probably meant it, at least at the moment.

They walked over to the door, and Jeremy looked down at her for a moment in silence. "Those eyes are going to haunt me. You know that, don't you?"

She forced herself to smile.

"Oh, Emily," he groaned, pulling her into his arms and searching blindly for her mouth.

Emily couldn't remember ever experiencing such an explosive mixture of pleasure at his touch and sadness that she would never have a reason to see him again. All of her safe and sane attitudes toward life seemed to shimmer around her, then dissipate into nothing. They were no longer real; Jeremy was.

His kiss seemed to be filled with a quiet desperation, as though he wanted her to remember his touch, his taste, the feel of him, as well as the sight and sound of him.

She slipped her hands beneath his jacket and slid her arms around his waist, feeling the tautness of his body against hers as she allowed herself the pleasure of touching him completely and totally. She pressed against him as though memorizing his body.

Emily could feel his heart's heavy thumping against his chest. His hand trembled when he slid it around the nape of her neck and restlessly massaged the tendons at the back of her skull.

"Oh, Emily," he whispered raggedly a few moments later, "I can't leave you now. I just can't." His mouth found hers once again, and his tongue began to explore, to claim, to entice and to tantalize.

Emily softly touched the contours of his back, following the indentation of his spine and the taut muscles that ran alongside its length. Unthinking, she tugged on his shirt until she was able to place her hands on his bare skin, sighing with unconscious relief at the marvelous sensation she was experiencing at feeling his warmth.

Jeremy knew he had lost control of the situation. What he was feeling was too intense to be denied. He wanted Emily Hartman as he had never wanted another woman. What he was feeling was more than just physical desire. He wanted so much more and knew that with her, he could find it.

Her soft, gentle touch had set off explosive depth charges inside him. She held him as though she never wanted to let him go, which was fine with him! If he could keep her in his arms from now on, he could think of no sweeter occupation than to hold and love Emily.

She made no protest when he swept her up in his arms. He lifted his head and stared down at her. Emily's eyes were closed, and she was smiling, no doubt aware of how badly he wanted her. He knew what he had to do. What he must do. He had to leave her, let her go. He couldn't take advantage of her trust in him.

Slowly he carried her into the bedroom, where the bed had been turned back. With his chest hurting from the pain in his heart, he lowered her onto the bed.

"Don't leave," she whispered, her arms securely around his waist.

"Emily?"

Her eyes slowly opened, and she looked up at him imploringly. "Will you make love to me?" she asked softly, her face flushed.

"I'm afraid I'm going to have to or lose my sanity," he admitted with a catch in his voice.

Her smile melted his heart. "You'll have to tell me what to do," she admitted.

Jeremy began to shake with the intensity of what he was feeling. Her complete and utter trust in him almost unmanned him.

He tried for lightness. "Well," he drawled, "first off, we have too many clothes on." Since he was lying across her on the bed, he knew that she was aware just how aroused he was. He sat up and began to unbutton her blouse.

"Do you mind?"

He glanced at her in surprise. "Do I mind what?"

"Making love to me?"

He began to laugh. "You're acting as though I'm doing you a favor."

She reached up and began to unbutton his shirt. "Yes."

Jeremy stood up and shrugged off his jacket, then his shirt. With economical movements he removed his shoes, socks, and then reached for his belt.

Emily knew that she would remember this moment for the rest of her life. She refused to think about the number of times Jeremy might have been in a similar situation with someone else. Instead, she realized that for the first time in her life she had chosen the man with whom she wanted to experience this most intimate relationship, and that regardless of what anyone else might think, this was right for her.

She watched as he unfastened his belt and pants, amazed to see his fingers trembling.

"Don't you have any idea how much I want you?" he said, sitting down beside her once more. She reached up and ran her hand along his shoulder and down his muscular arm.

"Do you?" she asked wistfully.

"I haven't been able to sleep for the past two nights, just thinking about you and how it felt to wake up with you the other morning." While he talked, he coaxed her up into a sitting position and carefully removed her suit jacket, the blouse, and with a tenderness she had never known a man could possess, he unfastened her bra, pulling it slowly from her shoulders.

Emily felt beautiful under his regard. He leaned over and draped her clothes across a chair near the bed. Then he reached for the fastening to her skirt.

By the time he'd removed all her clothing, Emily felt as though she'd die if he didn't touch her again. He stretched out beside her, then leaned over and kissed her softly on the lips. His hand cupped her breast, and his knee nudged her legs apart enough to enter the warm area between her thighs.

"Don't be afraid of me," he whispered, raising his head slightly and staring down at her.

How could she possibly be afraid of such a magnificent man? His broad shoulders and muscled chest tantalized her, and she ran her hands over them restlessly, wanting to possess him in some way that she didn't know. What a beautiful man he was. The beauty was also in his eyes. They expressed so much—his tenderness, his caring, his integrity.

"I could never be afraid of you," she finally replied.

Her words seemed to release some restraint within him, and he began to kiss and caress her, exploring and loving her with an urgency that left her shaken. He left no place untouched by either his hands or his mouth. He placed tiny kisses all over her body while his hands seemed to know where to touch her to create the most quivering sensations.

By the time he moved over her, she was almost pleading with him to help her express all that she was feeling. Emily had never known that she could be aroused to such a degree. She had never allowed any man such liberties, and now she was glad that she had waited, because Jeremy Jones was a master musician playing her body as though it were the most treasured of instruments, finding the tones and notes that she'd never known herself capable of expressing.

He took his time, giving her body an opportunity to adjust to him. Jeremy had never felt such an intense need to share all that he was feeling with another person. He wanted her to understand how he felt, how much he appreciated what she had offered him.

He waited, and was rewarded for his patience. She slipped her hands along his jaw and placed kisses on his mouth, nose and eyelids. His mouth sought hers, and she sighed as she melted once more against him.

Emily felt lost in a sea of sensation as Jeremy initiated her into this most ancient of love rites. She found herself responding to him as though her body remembered what her mind might have forgotten. He responded to her every touch, and she was delighted to discover how quickly and easily she could please him.

Then something seemed to be happening to her—a feeling began to grow and expand within her until, with a shining burst of color, Emily's world seemed to burst into a radiant hue, cascading sparkles of light and energy around them. As though waiting for just such a signal, Jeremy seemed galvanized into an urgency of movement that resulted in a soft cry of release. He gathered her closer in his arms with a convulsive movement, then slowly lowered himself, moving so that most of his weight was on the bed beside her.

They lay there for a long time in silence. Emily could think of nothing that had happened to her during her entire life to compare with what she was experiencing at the moment—a sense of completeness, of wholeness, of well-being. And she had Jeremy to thank for helping her discover such a new aspect of life and its pleasures.

"I never meant this to happen," Jeremy murmured when he could catch his breath.

"I know. I managed to seduce you."

Her pleased surprise caught him off guard, and he began to laugh. "I never know what to expect from you."

"Don't feel badly about what happened, Jeremy. I don't."

"I've never lost control of myself like that before," he said with a grimace. "I don't understand my reactions to you. But then, I never have."

She began to stroke his back, enjoying the play of muscles. "You took time to protect me."

"Yes."

"Please don't let any doubts creep in about what has happened. Just know that I wanted it to happen, too. It was a mutual decision and choice. I don't want you feeling anything but pleasure at the memory."

He grinned, his face cuddled against her neck. "That isn't hard to do right at the moment." He eased away from her and sat up, running his hand through his hair.

Emily smiled at the rumpled effect and at the expression of relaxed contentment on his face. She realized that she'd never seen him look quite that way, not since she'd first met him. *He works too hard and he doesn't take enough time for himself.*

She'd given him this, she suddenly realized, pleased to know that she could help him in some way.

"I don't want to leave you," he admitted finally. "I'd like to stay here with you, sleep with you in my arms, wake up with you tomorrow." He paused, glancing around the room distractedly. "But I can't."

"I know."

He picked up his clothes and disappeared into the bathroom. She heard the shower running for a couple of minutes. When he reappeared, he was dressed in his shirt, pants and shoes, and was pulling on his coat.

She smiled at the picture he made. Emily knew that she would smile at anything at the moment. Tomorrow was soon enough to face reality. Tonight she was still caught up in the fantasy of the moment.

He leaned over and kissed her, a slow, possessive kiss that clearly marked the change in their relationship. "I'll see you soon. I don't know how, but somehow I'm going to see you again."

"That would be nice."

He rearranged the covers so that she was tucked in, then stroked her hair away from her face. He seemed to be studying her intently, as though memorizing every feature.

"I'll call you in the morning," he said, abruptly turning away.

She nodded sleepily and watched as he walked out of the room, then closed her eyes. Tomorrow was soon enough to think about what had happened and what it meant. Tonight all she wanted to do was to relive the joy of all the sensations she'd discovered by making love with Jeremy Jones.

Seven

When Emily awakened, early-morning sunlight poured through the large windows of the room—she had neglected to pull the drapes the night before.

The night before. Her thoughts tumbled around her as she recalled all that had happened.

Slowly rolling over, she snuggled her cheek into the pillow. She peeked at her wristwatch and knew she didn't have much time before she had to leave for the airport.

The phone rang, and she fumbled for the receiver.

"H'lo?"

"Good morning." Would the sound of that voice always affect her so strongly? If so, she was in a considerable amount of trouble, because that voice could be heard at the twist of most dials.

"Good morning, Jeremy," she said with a smile.

"Did you sleep all right?"

"Just fine."

"Do you have any idea how much I hated to leave you last night?"

"Did you?" she asked softly, curling into the pillow with the phone still at her ear.

"Are you sure you have to leave today?"

"Positive."

"Will you write?"

"If you'd like."

"I'd like."

She smiled to herself.

"May I take you to the airport?"

"I don't think that's a very good idea."

She could hear the amusement in his voice. "Afraid I'll get carried away at the airport with my goodbye kiss?"

"There is that," she said with a grin.

"Oh, Emily. You don't know what it means to me to have found you."

"I'm feeling the same way."

"At least I'm not suffering alone."

"No."

She heard a whispered conversation, then Jeremy said, "There's someone here who'd like to speak with you."

Emily waited and heard a young voice say "Emily?" uncertainly.

Her heart felt as though it swelled in her breast. "Good morning, Michelle."

"Emily, you know what?"

"What, darling?"

"We watched *Snow White* last night. It was scary!"

"It was?"

"Uh-huh. I dreamed about being in the woods, and it scared me so I crawled in bed with Daddy."

"You did?"

"Uh-huh. And he said it was just a dream and that nobody was going to get me."

"Of course they aren't, sweetheart."

"Emily?"

"Yes?"

"Are you going to come see me today?"

"I'm afraid not. I have to take a plane back home."

"Do you live far away?"

"Pretty far, I'd say."

"Can I come see you sometime?" Michelle asked wistfully, and Emily's eyes filled with tears.

"I would love to have you come to visit me. Patti, my niece, is just about your age, and she lives next door to me."

She heard Michelle excitedly asking Jeremy if she could visit Emily, but she couldn't hear his response. Then Michelle said, "Here's my daddy. Bye."

"Emily?"

"Yes?"

"There are now two of us who can hardly wait to see you again."

"I'm not complaining."

"I'll let you go so you don't miss your plane." He paused as though unsure of what to say. "Don't forget me," he finally murmured.

She laughed. "I don't think you need worry about that."

"Take care of yourself."

"You, too." She hung up the phone, smiling.

Emily wondered what happened if you really and truly believed in fairy tales. Was it possible that they could in fact come true?

By the time she'd been home for a few days, her visit to Nevada had taken on a dreamlike quality. She found herself experiencing wild mood swings, first of euphoria at what might become her future, and then despair that she should even consider that Jeremy had meant all that he had said to her.

When she was in a positive mood, she would relive all that had happened, excited that Michelle had liked her immediately, eager to hear from Jeremy, wondering if there was a possibility that they could work out a future that would be spent together.

On her downswing, she would remind herself that he was, after all, an entertainer, and entertainers were notorious for their loose life-styles and promiscuous ways.

At those times she would cringe with embarrassment that she could have possibly been so naive as to believe him.

At first her heart had leaped into her throat every time the phone rang, but eventually she realized that he wasn't going to call. As the days and weeks began to pass, Emily had to come to grips with the fact that, whatever his reasons, Jeremy hadn't tried to contact her.

She had found a card and sent it to him the first week, thanking him for his hospitality and for their time together.

He didn't reply.

Emily had given little thought to the way the radio station would promote her once she returned. Despite her lack of enthusiasm, they insisted on interviewing her and using some of the pictures that had been taken of her and of Jeremy while she was in Las Vegas.

For a few weeks after her return, Emily herself was treated like a celebrity of sorts, and once again she was reminded of how much she disliked public life. She was grateful when the flurry of attention died down and other things took over space in the news.

Trying to act nonchalant about her trip was easy with strangers. But with Terri it was more difficult, because her sister knew her so much better.

"I want to hear about each and every thing you did," Terri had stated on Emily's first night home. "By the way, that haircut is extremely becoming. I can't quite put my finger on what else is different. There's a glow about you."

"I had a great time."

"Okay. So, go on. And what happened?"

Emily gave an expurgated account of her visit, going into a great deal of detail regarding her day at the beauty salon, what it was like shopping for expensive clothing. Terri wasn't buying her evasiveness.

"What aren't you telling me?"

"I don't know what you're talking about."

"Jeremy Jones, that's what I'm talking about. You spent an entire evening with Jeremy Jones, and yet you've scarcely mentioned him."

"Oh. Well, that's because our evening was interrupted. His daughter flew in unexpectedly, and he needed to meet her plane."

"His daughter? Then he is married," Terri said with a sigh.

"Divorced."

Terri perked up. "Ahh."

"Not that his marital status had anything to do with my visit. Aren't you the one who pointed out that I didn't fly out there to marry him?"

"I know, I know. But a person can dream, you know. I mean, can you imagine what it would be like to be married to Jeremy Jones—to live that life?"

Emily tried not to think about that possibility. It was too soon, despite what had happened between them. Of course the subject had never been brought up between them. It was silly of her to even consider it.

"His first marriage didn't survive," she pointed out, as much for herself as for Terri. "It must be tough to be married to a celebrity."

As the weeks passed, Emily reminded herself over and over that it was just as well. In a way, he'd let her down easy, letting her imagine that he would call. Once in a while she would argue on his behalf, explaining that he was no doubt too busy to contact her, but she would quickly point out that a phone call didn't take much time out of a person's life.

The vacation did trigger some small changes in Emily. She had discovered the fun of shopping for new and different styles. She experimented with her hair and makeup and enjoyed watching people respond more to her as she became more responsive to them.

She began to join her co-workers for lunch rather than taking her own and eating at her desk. Emily became more aware of those around her and interested in their lives.

Had she always been so cut off from people? she wondered. She knew she felt different, and it was more than a new hairdo and new styles of clothing.

She had begun to feel and to take part in sharing what others felt. Her life seemed to have made some sort of shift that she had been unconscious of at the time, but now everything looked different to her.

Her trip had been a great topic of conversation at work for weeks after she returned. Now she was treated as the expert on Jeremy Jones. Clippings regarding Jeremy turned up on her desk as though people thought she would be interested in everything that appeared in print about him. Wherever she went, Emily noticed pictures of him, heard his voice singing one of his hits or saw something that reminded her of their time together.

She didn't need to be reminded, but knew better than to allow anyone to know how she felt. It took a great deal of discipline to hide her reaction when she returned from lunch one day to find a copy of a well-known scandal magazine lying on her desk.

The headlines carried a banner regarding the bitter custody feud between Jeremy Jones and his wife. A blurred picture of Linda carrying Michelle was juxtaposed with one of Jeremy on stage, singing into a hand-held microphone.

Emily found herself reading the text, despite every intention she had to ignore the sensationalism that seemed to surround Jeremy. Cutting through the verbiage, Emily discovered that the story was based on the fact that Linda had entered a famous drug-and-alcohol rehabilitation center in California. The rest of the story was a rehash of her marriage to Jeremy, their divorce and the recent battle over custody of their young daughter.

She shook her head. How sad that their personal lives had to be splashed all over the front of a magazine.

Now that almost a month had passed since she'd returned from Las Vegas, Emily felt that she was handling what had happened fairly well. She knew she wasn't the first person to fall for sincere-sounding words uttered at a particularly romantic moment, and she probably wouldn't be the last.

At least no one in her hometown knew what a fool she'd made of herself, thank God.

The phone was ringing when she let herself into the house one evening. Dropping the mail and her purse onto the kitchen table she reached for the phone.

"H'lo?"

"Emily, this is Jeremy. How have you been?"

She thought for a moment that her heart had decided to give up functioning, and then it began to race in her chest as though to make up for that skip. Fighting for a casualness she was far from feeling, Emily responded, "I'm fine, Jeremy."

There was silence after she spoke, as though he expected to hear more from her. When she didn't speak, he said, "I'm sorry I haven't called before now, but—"

"Please don't apologize, I understand. Actually I've been rather busy myself."

"But I wanted you to know—"

"Jeremy, please. There's really no need for explanations. It was nice of you to call. I'm sorry that I can't talk longer, but I have plans for the evening, and I need to get ready."

Her heart was pounding so loudly she could hardly hear anything else.

After another lengthy pause, Jeremy's voice sounded cool and distant. "I see. I didn't mean to intrude."

"Oh." She tried for lightness. "That's no problem. How's Michelle?"

"Actually she's handling things better than anyone expected."

"I beg your pardon?"

"She happened to be watching television the night Linda's attempted suicide was reported, which is pretty tough on a five-year-old."

"Oh, my God! Jeremy, I didn't know!"

"Yeah, well. It probably wasn't of general interest where you live. They played it up in Las Vegas because I spend most of my time there."

"I'm so sorry. How is Linda?"

"Uh—well, her attempt wasn't successful, but she's in pretty bad shape mentally and emotionally."

"I saw she'd been admitted into a sanatorium."

"Yes. She'd been in the hospital for several weeks before they'd release her to the rehab clinic. I've spent most of my time over there with her, trying to convince her she can get through this and that Michelle needed her."

No wonder he hadn't called her. She'd been wrapped up in her own little pity party and hadn't given a thought to what he might be going through.

"Look, I'm sorry I caught you at a bad time. I'm glad to know things are going all right for you. I just wanted to say hello."

"Oh, Jeremy, I'm so glad you called. I've really missed you."

"Have you?"

"I'm going to a movie tonight with a couple of women from work, otherwise I wouldn't be in such a rush—"

His voice sounded considerably lighter when he said, "I understand. I'm glad to know you aren't sitting at home all the time." He paused and said in a softer tone, "I'm also glad to know you missed me."

"Tell Michelle hello for me. I hope she's adjusting to everything that's happened."

"So do I. Only time will tell. I'll let you go and try to call again soon. It looks as though my schedule is going to be changing. Henry's talking about a six-city tour. I've been arguing against it, but I'm not sure whether I'm going to win."

"I know you're busy, Jeremy. I understand."

"Just know that I think of you, and I'll stay in touch as well as I can under the circumstances."

"Thank you for calling me."

"It was my pleasure."

Emily hung up the phone and stood there staring at it. He had called her. He hadn't forgotten about her. She began to smile, then to laugh. Jeremy had called!

She spun around to call Terri, then paused. Wait a minute. What could she tell Terri, after all? Wouldn't she have to explain why he'd called her? Did she want Terri to know how excited she was that Jeremy Jones had actually called her, just to say hello?

Forcing herself to calm down, she hurried to take her shower, so she wouldn't be late meeting her friends. Emily felt happier than she had since she'd returned home. Whatever else happened, at least she knew that she could believe him.

Two weeks later, Emily was late getting home. She was so tired she felt as though she could sleep for a week. Terri met her at the door.

"Hi? What are you doing here?" Emily said, reaching for her key.

"I saw you drive up and thought I'd keep you company. Mike took Patti over to his mother's for dinner to give me a rest."

"Why didn't you go with them?" Emily asked, sinking into the first chair she got to.

"Mike thought I'd like to take a break from motherhood," Terri explained with a grin. "So I thought maybe we could go to a movie, or something. But when you didn't come home I began to wonder..."

"I stayed to get some end-of-the-month reports finished so I wouldn't have to work over the weekend." Emily sighed. "I think it might have been just as well if I had planned to work tomorrow. As it is, I'll probably sleep through the day just to recuperate."

Terri looked at her sister with concern. "You never learn when to stop pushing yourself, do you?" Shaking her head, she said, "Why don't you take a nice, long bath. I'll make you hot tea and soup or something."

"Oh, Terri, you're such a love. This is supposed to be your night off. You don't need to do that."

Terri shrugged. "I know, but frankly any conversation that is intellectually above four years old would be a welcome relief. Go on and fill your tub. I'll bring you your tea as soon as it's ready."

Emily stood and stretched, her hands going to the small of her back. "You managed to convince me, you silver-tongued rascal." Throwing her arms around Terri, she said, "What would I ever do without you?"

"I don't intend to give you the opportunity to find out." She squeezed Emily's shoulders and smiled. "Enjoy."

By the time Terri appeared with the steaming mug, Emily was gratefully ensconced in foamy bathwater. Handing her the cup, Terri sat down on the vanity bench to visit.

Terri could always be depended upon to share a humorous incident of her day, and Emily had come to treasure their daily visits. She was chuckling at one of Patti's latest antics some time later when they heard a knock at the front door.

"Expecting someone?" Terri queried.

Emily shook her head. "Not unless it's the paper-boy. It's time for him to be making his rounds."

"I'll pay him," Terri said, hopping up. "No need for you to give up your soak."

"Thanks. My purse is on the table," she added, hoping Terri heard her. If not, she'd probably see it there, herself.

Emily closed her eyes, feeling downright deca-dent—being waited on by her sister, sipping hot tea in a marvelously warm bubble bath. She heard Terri hurrying down the hallway toward her and smiled. She probably couldn't find Emily's purse.

"Emily!"

"My purse is—" Emily paused and slowly sat up in the tub. Terri's eyes looked twice their normal size. "Terri? What's wrong?" She'd never seen that look on Terri's face before. "Who is it?"

"I—I—I—I c-can't believe i-i-it's—" Her teeth were almost chattering, and she was pointing over her shoulder as though trying to explain by sign lan-guage.

Emily didn't know what was wrong, but she real-ized something drastic had happened. She started to stand up when she heard heavy footsteps down the hall.

"Who is it?" she hissed, sliding down under the bubbles once again and frantically motioning for Terri to close the door.

"Hello, Emily," came a voice that Emily hadn't expected to hear at her bathroom door.

"It's J-Jeremy Jones!" Terri managed to say in a harsh croak.

"Jeremy!" Emily didn't know whether to jump out of the tub or slide all the way under the water. "What are you doing here!"

"Looking for you," he said with a grin. He leaned against the door frame and crossed his arms. "Guess I found you, huh?"

"Would you get out of here!" she said, feeling as though her face would outshine a neon flashing light.

Jeremy nodded toward Terri. "You must be Emily's sister." he stuck out his hand. "I'm Jeremy Jones."

Terri's head bobbed up and down like a puppet on a string. "I—I know who you are, Mr. Jones. I'm Terri Thompson, and I'm one of your biggest fans. I just can't believe that you're—" She spun around and looked at Emily with an accusing stare. "You never told me he was coming here. Why didn't you say something?"

"She didn't know, Terri. I'm afraid it was a spur-of-the-moment decision. I was at the Dallas airport, supposed to be catching a flight to Atlanta. They announced the boarding of a plane to Little Rock, and I decided to catch it." He grinned down at Emily. "Henry's a little perturbed with me. I've got a concert in Atlanta tomorrow night."

The two women stared at him in varying degrees of shock. After noting their reaction, he shrugged. "So I can't stay long. I just wanted to stop in and say hi."

Terri looked over at Emily. "Is he serious?"

Emily was busy stirring the water around her, since her bubble bath seemed to be dissipating. "How would I know? He's here, isn't he?"

Terri took in his lounging figure, from well-shod toe to immaculately cut hair and nodded. "Either that, or I'm hallucinating."

Jeremy laughed. "Well, ladies. I will be a gentleman and wait in the other room until bath time is over." He straightened and then paused. "Unless, of course, you need someone to scrub your back..." he said with a wicked look in his eyes.

"I can manage just fine without you, but thank you all the same," Emily said with as much dignity as she could manage. As soon as he started down the hallway, she hissed, "Close the door, Terri!"

Terri had been standing there as though she were a statue waiting to be placed in a garden. At Emily's words she sprang toward the door, slammed it and fell against it. "My God, Emily. That was Jeremy Jones. And he's here! Right here in Little Rock. I can't believe it. I just can't—" She spun away from the door and stared at Emily. "Just what is going on between the two of you? And don't tell me nothing," she said as Emily opened her mouth, "because I will not believe it. My God! Anyone caught between the looks you two were giving each other would get singed." She grabbed a towel and handed it to Emily as she crawled out of the tub. "I think you may have forgotten to tell me everything that happened while you were in Las Vegas, little sister."

Emily hastily dried herself and fumbled for her housecoat. "Not now, Terri. I've got to find some clothes to wear. Go make some coffee or something. And didn't you have some soup heating?''

Reluctantly Terri opened the door. "You can't tell me he decided to stop over and pay you a surprise visit just because you won that contest.''

"Terri. I honestly don't know why he stopped by. You heard him. He's probably telling the truth. You know how crazy entertainers are.''

"I'm beginning to," she muttered, disappearing down the hall.

Now that Terri was gone, Emily could finally face what had just happened. Jeremy Jones had come to see her. He was there, right down the hallway from her, and she was going to have to pretend that she didn't want to throw herself into his arms and kiss him senseless.

He was crazy to have come. There was no question of that. But, oh! She was so glad he had. Dashing into her bedroom she grabbed the first thing she could find to put on—a pair of jeans and a sweatshirt. Hastily stuffing her feet into a pair of worn slippers, she started down the hallway.

She could hear Jeremy's voice coming from the kitchen. "Oh, didn't Emily tell you? I told her the last time I called that I would try to see her when I could. My schedule's been so hectic lately that I had no idea when that might be.''

"Thanks a lot, Jeremy," she muttered to herself. She knew she was in trouble as soon as she walked into the kitchen and saw Terri's accusing stare. So much for keeping your private life private, at least in this family, she thought.

For the next hour Jeremy regaled both women with stories about the band and past tours that had them howling with laughter. Emily totally forgot about how tired she'd been, and Terri sparkled with new energy.

Terri had discovered that Jeremy hadn't eaten and had quickly grilled him a steak, thrown together a tossed salad and microwaved a baked potato. Emily was content to enjoy the soup and watch Jeremy eat as though he hadn't seen food in several days.

It was marvelous to see him again. She had forgotten how much she enjoyed watching how his eyes changed expression. His flashing smile caused her stomach to flip, and she was grateful that she hadn't tried to eat more.

After finishing his meal, he sipped his coffee and absently reached for Emily's hand. Taking it in his, he rubbed it against his cheekbone, as though unaware of the intimate gesture. She didn't look at Terri. There was no going back now. Whatever his intentions, he was making it clear that he was staking a claim and didn't care who knew it.

As for Emily, she no longer cared what Terri thought. She was too caught up in the feel of his cheek against her knuckles. Every time he looked at her, she felt as though she'd received an electrical jolt, and the tingling that coursed through her body caused her to tremble.

A pause in the conversation came, and Terri looked up at the clock. "Oh, no. I didn't realize how late it was! Mike's probably been home for hours." She jumped up and looked at Jeremy and Emily sitting side by side, Emily's hand still in Jeremy's.

"Uh, well. I've got to run. It was certainly great visiting with you, Jeremy. I'd like to say that Emily's told me so much about you. However, that would certainly be a lie."

Jeremy grinned, enjoying the flush on Emily's cheeks. He let go of her hand and got to his feet. "I'm very pleased to meet you, too, Terri. I have a feeling we'll be seeing a great deal of each other in the coming months."

Terri smiled. "I have a feeling that you're probably right." The look she gave Emily made it clear that she was going to be demanding some explanations at their next private meeting!

Emily stood while Jeremy let Terri out the door with a wave, then carefully closed and locked it behind her. Then he turned around and just looked at her.

"I suppose you're wondering what I'm doing here," he said after a few moments.

"It sounds as though you've been really busy."

"I have been. I've got five shows to put on in the next two months. The one tomorrow night is being televised to be replayed on cable next month."

"That's great, Jeremy."

"A few years ago I would have thought so, too. But not now."

She walked over to him. "Why?"

"Because my life's too hectic now. I don't have any time for a personal life."

"Yes, I'm sure Michelle misses you when you're on the road."

He reached out and took her hands and pulled them to his chest. "I'm not talking about Michelle at the moment. You see, I've discovered something rather strange has happened to me.''

She felt as though she would turn into a shooting flame under the look he was giving her at the moment. "What's that?'' she managed to say.

"I seem to have fallen in love with you.''

"Oh, Jeremy," she said, and leaned against his chest. She could feel his heart pounding so that his chest shook with each beat. He slid his arms around her and held her close against his breast.

"You're in my head everywhere I go. All of my songs seem to be written to you, for you, about you. I hear your voice, and I think you're there with me. I can't go to sleep at night without dreaming about you.''

Her laugh sounded very shaky in her ears. "Sounds a little strange at that.''

"I don't suppose you've been suffering from similar symptoms, have you?''

Funny he should ask. "It may only be a temporary condition that you'll overcome shortly," she responded, sidestepping his question.

"Somehow I doubt it.''

Emily realized that tears were rolling down her cheeks.

"So what I was wondering," he said in a carefully casual voice, "was what you'd think about marrying me?''

"Oh, Jeremy, I don't know how to handle this.''

"Do you think I do? I've been walking into doors and walls ever since you left. I was hoping you could put me out of my misery.''

She hadn't looked up. "It's so soon. How could we possibly know each other well enough? I don't know what to say."

"Just answer one question, please."

She nodded, still without looking at him.

"Do you love me?"

How could she lie to him? Leaning back so that she could see his face, his wonderful, strained-looking face, she slipped her hands up so that she cupped his jaw and said, "Of course I love you. How could I possibly resist you?"

Eight

With a groan, Jeremy leaned down and kissed her as though starving for the taste and feel of her. His hands swiftly skimmed across her back and down to her hips. He pressed her against his hard length, silently showing her the effect she had on him.

Jeremy lifted her so that her toes were barely touching the floor. He'd leaned against the door, his feet slightly apart, so that her weight was resting against him. His mouth found hers in such a searing kiss that she felt as though she were going to burst into flames.

When she finally managed to pull away from him long enough to breathe, she began, "I don't think—"

"Good. Neither can I. All I know is that I love you." He gave her a short, hard kiss. "I want you."

He kissed her again. "And I need you so badly I ache with it."

He held her for a moment as though trying to gain some control over his emotions, then picked her up and started down the hallway. Without turning on a light, he carried her to the bed. Laying her gently on the mattress, he began to remove his clothes, never taking his eyes off her.

Once bare he stretched out beside her, his fingers searching for the snap on her jeans. With economical movements he removed her jeans, sweatshirt and shoes.

"You do that like an expert," she whispered.

"No. Like a suffering man who's desperate," he corrected, sliding his heated body alongside hers with a sigh. "Oh, you feel so good, Emily. And I've missed you so much. You have no idea."

She was beginning to get an inkling. She felt his body tremble as he pulled her into his arms. His leg came across hers as though to hold her to him as tightly as possible.

So this was what heaven was all about. Being with the one person in all the world who made you feel whole and complete.

Now that he held her in his arms, Jeremy seemed to relax a little. He began to stroke her—soft, gentle strokes, as though he were enjoying the fact that at last he was with her and could hold and love her.

The words he murmured, the suggestions he made, combined to set off tingling charges of sensation throughout her body.

"God, I've missed holding you," he whispered while he nibbled on her earlobe. He trailed kisses across her cheek, over her nose, on each eyelid. "Surely you must feel it, too."

"Feel what?" she managed to say in a ragged tone of voice.

"The magic we create when we're together. What I'm feeling is too powerful to be all one-sided."

Stroking her hand down the long length of his back, Emily knew that she couldn't deny what he was asking. "It isn't one-sided," she admitted.

Her words seemed to shoot through him like a surge of adrenaline, and he found he could no longer restrain his need for her. Moving over her, he took possession of her body as he hoped to take possession of her heart. She had to love him, because he knew that he desperately needed her in his life.

Emily discovered that her memories were no comparison to having Jeremy in her arms once more. She had forgotten how he felt so close to her, and how he made her feel. She clung to him, encouraging him with every beat of her heart, every breath she took, to share this marvelous experience.

Jeremy expressed his love physically, showing her in every way he knew that they were good together, that they belonged together. His rhythmic lovemaking caught them both up in the moment, shattering all thought, causing them to suddenly find themselves in another world of total bonding, where each was the natural completion of the other.

They clung to each other after Jeremy had slumped limply by her side, still holding her tightly against him.

He refused to consider her possible refusal of his earlier suggestion.

Jeremy knew that now he had found her, he was not going to let her go.

Eventually he stirred. "I sincerely hope that was a yes," he managed to say, and Emily smiled.

"I have to admit that you do have a rather persuasive manner that I find almost irresistible."

"Almost?"

Emily lay with her head on his shoulder. Their arms and legs were still entwined. "I do love you, Jeremy," she said softly.

"Why do I hear an unspoken *but* in there?" he murmured.

"I just don't think we should rush into anything."

He glanced down at the two of them and grinned. "You don't, huh?"

"I mean, how can you be so sure that we could make a marriage work?"

"Because I have faith in our ability to work out whatever problems might crop up."

She was quiet, and after a moment, he said, "You really don't care for my life-style, do you?"

"It's just that I'm a private person, and I don't like my personal life splashed around gossip columns."

He sighed. "Why couldn't I have fallen for a woman who gloried in seeing her name and face in print?"

"Good question."

"The point is, I'm in love with you, and I don't want to spend my life commuting to Little Rock in order to be with you."

"And do you always get your way?"

"You'd better believe it," he said with a grin, watching her face for a reaction.

"It's scary to think about."

"What is?"

"Marrying you—becoming a part of your life."

"Oh, that. To me the scariest thing would be not to marry you and not have you as part of my life." They lay there together for several moments without speaking. Finally he said, "Besides..."

When he didn't continue, she asked, "Besides what?"

"You lured me on with your delectable beauty, your intelligence, your luscious body. You seduced me, Emily, remember? It's only fair that you do the honorable thing and marry me."

"You're crazy."

"I'm beginning to believe it. Here I am in Little Rock when I'm supposed to be in Atlanta!" Rolling over onto his back so that she was lying on top of him, he said, "I'll tell Henry that you bewitched me and I had no choice."

Even in her wildest fantasies Emily had never imagined that Jeremy Jones would be there in her bed, much less discussing marriage.

"When do you intend to leave?"

"Are you trying to get rid of me?"

She shifted so that her body slid along his. "What do you think?"

"I think you're driving me out of my mind," he said, pulling her head down to his.

There was no more conversation and very little sleep for either one of them that night.

"Emily, love, wake up." She stirred sleepily. "Darling, I hate to wake you, but would it be possible for you to get me to the airport? I really do need to leave."

Emily sat up with a start, suddenly realizing that those delicious dreams she'd been savoring had not been dreams at all. Jeremy was there with her.

The windows were only a few shades lighter than the rest of the room. The sun hadn't risen. She glanced at her watch. It was still early, but not if Jeremy had to be in Atlanta.

She glanced around and saw him sitting on the edge of the bed, fully clothed, watching her with a tender smile. "I'm sorry. You should have awakened me earlier."

"I didn't dare. I needed to be showered and dressed before I woke you up. Otherwise, I would never leave."

Emily stretched and ran her hand through her hair. Although neither of them had slept much, she, for one, felt wonderful. Leaning over, she gave him a quick kiss, then she slipped out of bed.

"I'll be with you in a few minutes," she said, disappearing down the hallway to the bathroom.

By the time she had showered and dressed, Jeremy had made coffee. He was leaning against the kitchen cabinet when she walked into the room. "I called the airport," he said. "Luckily I can catch a flight out of here in an hour."

"I'm glad. I wouldn't want your detour to have created problems for you."

He draped his arm around her and pulled her close against him. "The only problem I have at the moment is getting you to agree to marry me."

"I want to very much, Jeremy. You must know that. I just think we need some time."

"All right. I'll give you all the time you need. In the meantime, I consider myself engaged."

"But not publicly, please."

"What do you mean?"

"I would just like some time to get used to the idea, that's all."

"Look, I know how you feel about all the publicity. I can understand it. And if my plans work out, you won't have to be subjected to it as much in the future."

"What do you mean?"

"Remember I told you about writing the musical score for a movie? They like it and intend to use it. In the future I'd like to spend more of my time composing and less time with public appearances."

"Are you sure? You aren't saying that as a way to placate me?"

"I'm saying it because that's what I want. There's no reason that we can't spend a large portion of our time here if you prefer that."

"How will Michelle feel about all of this?"

He grinned. "As a matter of fact, she's been insisting that we come to visit you. It seems that Matilda misses you."

"Matilda? Her punk rocker doll?"

"The very one."

Emily laughed. "I see. Michelle hasn't missed me, but Matilda has."

"You got it."

"Oh, Jeremy, she's such a love."

"Just think. You take me, you get her, too. Now that's quite a deal, wouldn't you say?"

"I couldn't possibly pass up such a combination."

He put his cup down and enfolded her in his arms. "Thank God. I don't want to think about not having you in my life. Michelle and I both need you, Emily."

"I need you, too, you know."

"Convince me."

She went up on her toes and kissed him, loving the feel of him, the spicy scent of him. Her heart felt as though it would burst with love.

When she finally drew away, her breathing was ragged. He took a deep breath and said, "I've got to go. Now. Or we're going to end up back in bed."

Later, on the way to the airport, Jeremy outlined his schedule to her for the next three months. "I don't see how I'll be able to get back to see you before then, but I'll try. In the meantime, I'll call as often as I can."

They pulled up in front of the airport, and Jeremy leaned over and gave her a brief kiss.

"Take care of yourself," she said, trying to hold back tears until she was alone.

"Always. I'll see you as soon as I can."

True to his word, Jeremy called whenever possible. Sometimes it was quite late, waking her up, but Emily never cared. She began to watch the magazines for anything published about him, as though in some way she could feel closer to him.

Her biggest surprise was Michelle's call.

"Where are you, honey?" Emily asked as soon as Michelle identified herself.

"I'm at home. Cynthia has been staying here with me since Daddy is gone."

"I bet you miss him, don't you?"

"Uh-huh, but he calls me every morning."

"Good for him."

"And he told me that you really are going to come live with us."

"He told you that?"

"Uh-huh, and said I could call you whenever I wanted to. So I did."

"I see." Emily smiled. Jeremy wasn't going to let her back out, not if he could help it.

"Can I come see you? Matilda misses you very much."

"So I heard."

"She says she can come to see you on the airplane."

"I suppose she could."

"I could bring her."

"Well, that would be up to your daddy, wouldn't it?"

"If you asked him, he'd let me, I think."

"But you couldn't come by yourself. There are no direct flights between here and there."

"Oh."

"But maybe your daddy will bring you to see me, soon."

Michelle sounded quiet. "Maybe. But he's so busy."

"I know he is, honey."

"But soon he's not going to travel, and then we can all be together. Won't that be fun?"

"I think it sounds like lots of fun, myself."

"Me, too. Cynthia says I have to hang up now," she said all in the same breath. "Can I call you again?"

"Of course you can. I love hearing from you."

"I'm glad you're going to come live with us."

"So am I, sweetheart. So am I."

Emily tried to keep her life on as even a keel as possible, considering that she was agreeing to a total lifestyle change. No one at the office knew that Jeremy had been to see her or that he frequently called her.

Terri, on the other hand, took credit for the entire relationship once she'd recovered from her surprise.

Emily kept feeling that she was dreaming, but if so, she didn't want to wake up.

Then one day there was a special interview in a leading news magazine featuring Linda Jones. Someone had left the magazine on her desk, turned to the article. Emily found it when she returned from lunch. She sank slowly to her chair and began to read.

The interview told about Linda's bout with drugs and alcohol, her attempted suicide and the several weeks she spent at the rehabilitation center.

It was a moving story, and Emily was impressed with Linda's honesty regarding what had happened to her, and the possible reasons why. It was obvious that Linda had begun to get in touch with herself in an effort to find answers for her behavior.

The accompanying pictures showed a happy, healthy-looking woman, a far cry from the blurred print last spring.

As she neared the end of the article, Emily stiffened. The reporter had questioned Linda regarding her present relationship with Jeremy.

"Yes, Jeremy has been extremely supportive during all of this. We're very close. He and our daughter Michelle visited me regularly while I was recuperating. I really don't know what I would have done without him these past few months. He's always been there whenever I needed him."

The article ended with these words:

When asked if there was a possibility of a reconciliation between her and the famous singer, Ms. Jones just smiled and said it was too soon to be making any announcements on that subject. However, from what I observed, there was little doubt that someone had put a sparkle in Linda's eyes. Who better than the father of her only child?

Who, indeed? Emily thought, after carefully placing the magazine back on her desk.

He had loved Linda; she was Michelle's mother. There was no reason why he shouldn't have spent time with her and encouraged her in her recovery.

They had never discussed Linda, it was true, but then most of his calls had been hurried. And what about Michelle? Surely Jeremy wouldn't have encouraged his daughter to call Emily if there was a chance that he and Linda were getting back together.

She had to stop playing guessing games. She reminded herself of her earlier reactions when he hadn't called her. If she didn't watch out, she would create another crisis between them.

Jeremy loved her. He had told her so, and she believed him. She would continue to believe him until he explained otherwise. If anyone was to blame for the present situation, she was. Jeremy had made it clear that he wanted the world to know he was engaged.

She had been the one who asked him to wait until after his tour to announce their plans. And he was definitely making plans. Every time he called, he teased her about the time he intended to take for his honeymoon. Some of the exotic locales he suggested surprised Emily. She had to keep reminding herself that money would no longer be the deciding factor on where she went and where she lived.

Emily appreciated Jeremy's willingness to give her this time to get used to the idea of being his wife. She couldn't become suspicious because he'd given her the space, no matter what was said in a magazine.

Feeling as though she'd fought a tremendous battle and won, Emily began to work again. Things would turn out well for them. She just needed to have some faith and trust in Jeremy.

As soon as she got home that evening, Terri came racing over from next door. "Guess what?"

"I'm fresh out of guesses. Tell me."

"Jeremy's special is supposed to be on cable tonight."

"Oh, that's right. I'd forgotten he said it was going to be televised. What time does it come on?"

"Ten o'clock. Do you want to come over to watch it?"

"Not tonight, but thanks."

"Suit yourself. See you later." Her sister gave her a friendly wave and dashed back home.

Emily smiled, almost envying her the energy. She hadn't realized how stressful being in love and preparing to start a whole new life could be.

She found herself waking up nights from disturbing dreams, dreams where Jeremy was surrounded by crowds of people, where she could not get close to him.

When the special started, she knew that her dreams were not that far off base. The camera panned the huge coliseum where he was performing, and she was appalled at the size of the crowd. All those people were there to see him, to cheer him on.

Watching the show made her realize how much she missed him. If there had ever been a doubt in her mind that she loved him and wanted to be a part of his life, those doubts disappeared at the sight of him.

The close-ups made her heart lurch in her breast. She had only seen him dressed for a performance that one time in Las Vegas. His stage costumes were impressive and emphasized his lithe build and catlike grace. No wonder the women were screaming in ecstasy, she thought, smiling to herself.

Jeremy Jones had it all—talent, looks, charisma and a gentleness of spirit that radiated around him. No wonder everyone loved him. He was so easy to love.

Seeing him brought an ache to her chest. She had missed him so much. Each song he sang spoke to her as though the words had come from her heart. If he had indeed been thinking of her when he wrote them, she could not possibly question how he felt about her.

During a break in the performance, a special backstage interview that had been filmed a few weeks after the concert, came on. Jeremy and the reporter had chatted informally at the hotel where he was staying.

Jeremy hadn't told her about this part of the interview. He looked tired, although his tousled hair and casual clothes gave him added appeal.

Jeremy was candid with the reporter and admitted that he hoped to retire from the travel end of the business. When asked about his personal life, Jeremy was deliberately vague, yet hinted that there was someone special in his life. Refusing to respond to speculation, he laughed at the reporter's inquisitiveness and explained that he considered his personal life private.

He was doing that for her, Emily knew, and she loved him for it. She was becoming aware that what was being said about him was not important. It was who he was that counted.

She had allowed her mind to drift away from the interview, but was brought back to what was happening on the screen when someone joined Jeremy on the sofa.

It was Linda.

Emily felt as though she'd been hit in the stomach with a doubled fist. What was Linda doing there?

She looked even better on television than she'd appeared in the magazine, wearing a figure-hugging knit dress and a radiant smile.

Emily heard the reporter say, "I understand you flew in today to see Jeremy and agreed to join us during this segment of the program." When she agreed, giving Jeremy a sparkling glance, the reporter continued, "Tell me, Linda, how—"

Emily could no longer hear anything from the television because her pulse was pounding heavily in her ears. She stared at the television screen as the camera moved from one to the other as they laughingly conversed with the interviewer. She began to shake, feeling as though she were coming down with a hard chill.

Why hadn't Jeremy told her about the interview? Why had he not mentioned that Linda had flown in to see him? And why? Why had Linda felt it necessary to flaunt their relationship? There was no denying the bond between the two people. It had showed when Linda greeted Jeremy. It had showed when he returned her smile with a warm handclasp.

Emily felt betrayed...left out...overlooked...lied to.

When the second segment of the concert came on, she got up and turned off the television. No more. She couldn't take any more of Jeremy Jones. Her head throbbed with every heartbeat, and she wandered into the kitchen to make a cup of tea.

She lost track of time as she sat at the kitchen table and sipped her tea. Her mind felt paralyzed. When the phone rang an hour or so later, she answered it like an automaton.

"Were you asleep?" Jeremy asked.

She wasn't ready to talk with Jeremy. Dear God, but his timing couldn't be worse. "No."

"You sound tired. Are you okay?"

"I think tired could pretty well sum up how I feel." She felt numb; she didn't want to feel. Not ever. Feeling brought pain. She wasn't sure she could handle the pain at the moment. Perhaps after a good night's rest she'd be better able to understand her reaction. Not now. Please. Not now.

"Tomorrow's the last concert. I expect to go home and crash for a few weeks."

"I can understand that. I'm sure you'll be glad to get back to Michelle."

"You'd better believe it. Did you see the show on cable tonight?"

"I—uh. Yes. Yes, I saw it."

"So, what did you think?"

"About the show, or about Linda?"

There was a moment of surprised silence. "What about Linda?"

"You didn't tell me that Linda had come to see you."

Another pause. "Nooo. I don't suppose I did, at that."

"I understand. After all, she's Michelle's mother, and she was your wife, and . . ."

"And?"

"Nothing. I, uh, was just surprised that she was there."

"If you saw the show then you know why she was there. She was very candid, which rather surprised me."

But Emily hadn't heard what she said. She'd only watched them together. And she'd heard over and over in her head what Linda had told the magazine reporter. Was Emily the last to know what everyone had already accepted?

"Emily? Are you there?"

"Yes."

"Look. I know it's late, and I won't keep you. I was wondering if you'd meet me in Vegas this weekend. I should get back over there in a couple of days. And we have some plans to make."

"Do we?"

"Emily, dammit! What is with you tonight? You're acting as though we hadn't already made plans to announce our engagement as soon as the tour was over. The tour will be over tomorrow night. I've been as patient as I know how."

"Yes. Yes, you have. The thing is, Jeremy, I'm not at all sure I can go through with this at the moment. Why don't you call me when you get back to Vegas? We'll talk then."

"But, Emily—"

"Tell Michelle hello for me. Give her a hug. I'll talk to you later."

"Later! Don't leave it like this. Tell me what's wrong. Share with me whatever's bothering you."

"I can't, Jeremy. Not just yet. Give it a few days. I've got to go now."

She heard him faintly say "Emily!" as she hung up the phone.

Carefully washing out her cup, Emily turned out the light and went into her bedroom. Jeremy's poster still hung on the wall. She stood in front of it and studied the man she loved.

The problem wasn't Jeremy; she was the problem, and she knew it. Emily couldn't accept and really believe that Jeremy Jones was in love with her and wanted to marry her.

How had Cinderella really felt when Prince Charming found her and insisted on taking her back to his palace for a happy-ever-after existence? Had she had any doubts regarding her ability to make him happy? Had she ever wondered if he truly loved her or whether she had offered him a challenge he couldn't resist?

Emily's short laugh was without humor. She certainly hadn't been much of a challenge to Jeremy. She'd fallen right into his arms from the very beginning, his for the taking.

Linda hadn't been able to cope with being married to him. Why did Emily think she could do any better? What made her think she had the wisdom and knowledge to build a strong, healthy relationship with him?

She'd always been a loner. She really didn't know how to relate to people. Somehow Jeremy had known how to draw her out of herself. She had opened up with him. Felt safe and loved with him. But what did she have to offer in return?

She couldn't think of a thing that any of his many worshiping fans couldn't offer as well. She loved him,

but was her love strong enough to bridge the gap between their different personalities and life-styles?

She didn't want to face the answer.

Nine

Emily went through all the motions at work the next day, but later she could not remember what she'd done. People spoke to her, and she must have responded sensibly because they went about their business.

Several mentioned in passing the concert that had been on cable television, but when she had no comment, they went on. Thank God no one knew that Jeremy had asked her to marry him. How could she have faced people each day if they thought she was foolish enough to have believed he meant it?

Of course he meant it, her inner voice pointed out. *Jeremy is an honorable man.*

He may have meant it at the time, while he was going through the turmoil with Linda. But Linda is so much better now. He has more to consider than just your feelings, she reminded herself. And even if he did want to marry her, how would she be able to cope with the knowledge that Linda had a right to be in his life because she was Michelle's mother?

Her recognition that she was jealous of the other woman made her ill. But at least she had finally faced the truth about her reactions. All of her excuses and temporizing had finally boiled down to the fact that she felt threatened by Jeremy's relationship with Linda.

Until she could come to terms with her feelings, she couldn't allow herself to make any plans for a marriage. Not only was her future happiness at stake, but so was Jeremy's and Michelle's. Michelle loved her mother. Even if Jeremy continued to have custody, Linda would have some part in her child's life. If Emily couldn't accept that fact, there was no reason to allow her relationship with Jeremy to continue.

Emily was almost relieved when one of the women mentioned that she had to leave early for an emergency dental appointment. It gave Emily an opportunity to volunteer to stay late and help get the reports done. She still found an escape in working with numbers. They were so dependable, so exacting. She didn't have to deal with fluttery, inexact emotions that could suddenly swamp her with their intensity.

For a little while, she could forget the unsureness of her life at the moment, as well as the decision that she knew she would have to make sooner or later.

Work had become a haven.

Hours later when she finally let herself into the house, she was so weary she wanted to drop. She turned on the light in the kitchen and stopped, her heart leaping.

Jeremy waited at the table.

Not now! Not tonight! I need time. I need to be ready for this!

She stood there and just stared at him.

He'd come to his feet when she walked in, his expression wary.

"How did you get in?" were her first words, and she could have cried at their lack of warmth. What she wanted to do was to throw herself into his arms and tell him how much she loved him, how much she missed him, and how very much she wanted to be his wife.

"Terri let me in. I hope I didn't startle you. I chartered a plane and left right after the performance tonight. It felt good to just sit here alone for a while, in the dark, and wait for you to come home."

"Oh." She couldn't think of anything else to say. He looked so tired, as exhausted as she felt.

Turning to the counter, she said, "I'll make us some coffee."

"Emily?"

She didn't turn around. "Yes?"

"What was all of that about last night on the phone? You scared the hell out of me."

"I didn't mean to."

He walked over and turned her around. "Aren't you even going to say that you're glad to see me?"

She closed her eyes, forcing the tears back, then opened them again. "I *am* glad to see you. I thought you were going directly to Las Vegas."

"That's what I intended, thinking you'd meet me out there. But when you wouldn't agree to that, I came here."

"Michelle needs you."

"I know that. You don't have to remind me." He tightened his grip on her shoulders. "I have needs, too, though, and you're one of them. If something's bothering you, then I want you to talk to me about it, dammit. I want to know what's wrong."

"Seeing Linda with you upset me."

"So I gathered."

"And I haven't come to terms with my feelings regarding the two of you."

"Whatever there is between Linda and me has nothing to do with you."

"At least you admit there's something there."

"Of course there is—Michelle. She's extremely important to both of us. Surely you can understand that!" He dropped her arms and paced across the room. "Then again, maybe you can't. You don't know what it's like to have a child."

"I can't deny that now, can I?"

"But there's no reason for you to be jealous of Linda. That was over years ago. I told you that."

"Reason doesn't have much to do with feelings. At the moment I don't seem to have any control over what I happen to be feeling."

"Are you going to let this come between us? Without even trying to deal with it? Are you going to retreat back into your own little world where nobody ever demands anything of you?"

"I don't know yet."

"Emily! Dear God! Don't do this to us. I know you love me. Don't let your insecurities drive a wedge between us!"

"To be honest, Jeremy, I'm really not in any condition to carry on this discussion tonight. I've just put in several grueling hours at work. I can't deal with what I'm feeling, how I'm feeling and why I shouldn't be feeling...not at the moment."

"Do you think you're the only person who keeps long hours and works hard? I can't even remember the last time I was in bed."

"Or who with," she blurted out, then covered her lips, appalled at what she'd said.

He stared at her as though unable to believe what she had just said. "You really believe that, don't you? That's what all of this is about. You're still judging me because I'm an entertainer and because of the reputation that goes with that profession."

"I don't know what I believe anymore, Jeremy. All I thought I was doing was flying out to Las Vegas for a publicity promotion. I didn't know my whole life was going to be turned upside down, inside out, that I'd become involved with someone—"

"Yes? Go ahead, someone—"

"All right. I didn't know I'd get involved with someone who was so famous, whose every word is quoted, whose ex-wife is famous because she *is* his ex-wife. I don't even know who I am anymore. At least here I have my own identity. If I marry you, I'll never know for sure who I am, or what I'm doing." She began to cry, and she hated herself for breaking down. She despised crying, in herself or in anyone else. Emily considered herself strong and independent. Tears were a sign of helplessness as far as she was concerned.

Furiously wiping her eyes, she muttered, "I hate to cry."

"It's more than that, Emily. You hate to feel. You hate to admit that you're human, just like the rest of us. You want everything to fit nicely into niches. Unfortunately feelings aren't made to be treated that way."

He spun around and walked toward the door. "You were right. I should have gone directly to Las Vegas. Even at five, Michelle understands what love is. Love doesn't place restrictions and conditions. The only important thing to Michelle is that I love her and I'm there for her. Maybe you should take lessons from her," he said, and walked out the door.

Emily stood there for a long while, not moving. He was gone. Jeremy had come to see her after almost two months, and she had neither hugged nor kissed him, never once expressed any joy at seeing him.

What had she done? Just how stupid could one woman be? She ran to the door and opened it, but the only thing in sight were the small red taillights of his car.

He must have rented a car, as well as chartered a plane. All of that just to see her. And she had treated him as though he were an uninvited salesman on cleaning day.

She realized that tears were continuing to pour down her cheeks. This time she didn't care. He'd been right, of course. She *was* afraid of feelings. She was so afraid of being hurt that she preferred not to feel at all. She loved him because of his warmth, his openness, his willingness to share himself. She loved him because he was so understanding of his daughter and her feelings. She even loved him because he continued to keep open the line of communication between himself and Linda, not for his sake, or even her sake, but because he understood the importance of their relationship for Michelle's sake.

Emily saw herself for the coward that she was. She knew that she didn't deserve Jeremy's love, but, oh, she wanted him to know that she wanted to learn more about that unconditional love he was talking about.

If he would give her the chance.

She called the airport, despite the late hour, and made a reservation to fly to Las Vegas the next morning. She intended to find Jeremy and ask his forgiveness for her behavior. He might not forgive her, but she would never forgive herself if she didn't ask him, face-to-face.

She spent most of the rest of the night packing, writing notes to the office and lying in bed, staring at the ceiling. She knew Jeremy had been angry when he left. Maybe by the time she got out there he would have had a chance to calm down, and they could talk.

When she finally fell asleep, her dreams were filled with turmoil. She felt as though she were trying to hurry but couldn't move, and she was frantic. She had to move, had to get there, had to explain—

The phone began to ring, waking her from a nightmarish feeling of being too late. Groping for the phone, she saw that it was almost six o'clock in the morning. Her alarm was due to go off any minute, in order to give her time enough to get ready to go to the airport.

"H'lo?"

"Emily! Oh, God, Emily!"

She sat up in bed. She had barely recognized Terri's voice. "Terri, what's happened? Is it Mike? Patti?"

"Oh, Emily. It's Jeremy! He— Oh, dear God, he's—"

"Jeremy!" A sense of foreboding rushed over her. Her dreams still seemed to swirl around her. "What is it?"

"His plane crashed sometime last night—somewhere near Las Vegas. I just heard it on the radio while I was making Mike's breakfast."

Her nightmares had become reality. "Is he dead?" Her voice didn't sound like her own.

"The radio didn't say. The details were sketchy. But a plane crash! So few people survive them. Remember that television star who was killed not too long ago!"

Emily could think of nothing but the fact that she had intended to fly out there this morning to see him. To explain. To explain what? What difference did it make now?

"Emily?"

"Yes."

"What are you going to do?"

"Do? I, uh, I don't know. I was supposed to fly out there this morning, but I—"

"Then go. At least you'll be out there."

"But now— I don't know what to do."

"I wonder what they've told his little girl?"

Michelle. Michelle who learned from television that her mother had attempted suicide. Would she also learn about her father's death the same way?

"I've got to go out there."

"Yes. I'll take you to the airport."

They were both crying but trying hard to get a grip on their emotions.

"Thanks." She replaced the phone and started to go to the closet. "He's not dead. I know he's not dead. I would know if he were gone. Something inside me would have died if he were gone. I just know he's all right. The reports are exaggerated. They might have had some problem and had to put down somewhere. There's probably nothing really serious. The news-people always blow everything up. Please, God, please. Let that be the case this time. Please let him be all right. Just let him be all right."

At least she had already laid out what she had planned to wear, so there were no decisions to make. Like a robot, Emily dressed and carried her bags outside. She wouldn't let herself think about the possibilities. She was going out there. She would get as close as she could to Jeremy, even if it was the last time.

Hoping for more details, Emily bought a paper at the Las Vegas airport and read it while she waited for her suitcase. Now that she was there, she wasn't sure where to go.

The headlines were stark. The plane had developed engine problems a few miles out of Las Vegas. The pilot had been forced to land. Both Jeremy and the pilot were listed in critical condition at the hospital.

He was alive. Dear God. He had survived the crash.

The hospital. He was at the hospital. Grabbing her bag, she hailed a cab.

Her heart sank when she saw the crowd around the hospital. Obviously she wasn't the only one trying to get word on Jeremy's condition. Why hadn't she thought of that? No one was going to believe her if she tried to explain who she was. How ironic that her strong desire for privacy should place her in such a position, now that she needed to see him, to know how he was.

"Emily! Thank God you're here!"

She spun around. Cynthia was coming across the street toward her.

"Oh, Cynthia. How is he?"

"He's out of surgery. They aren't allowing any visitors, but Dad's inside, waiting for any word. Come on. I'll show you where you can find the waiting room."

"How is Michelle?"

"We haven't told her. At least this time we made sure she didn't hear about it accidentally." Cynthia hugged Emily. "I should have known you'd be on your way as soon as you heard. Dad tried to call you, off and on, but couldn't get an answer and didn't know another way to reach you."

They entered a side door, well away from the crowded vestibule, and Cynthia led Emily down a series of hallways, until they came to a waiting room.

Henry jumped to his feet when he saw Emily at the door of the waiting room. "Thank God, you're here. I've been ringing your house for hours, but there wasn't any answer."

"I heard about it on the news. How is he?"

"Doc said he came through the surgery in fine shape. Had some internal injuries, broke his collarbone and his left arm. But barring complications, he's going to be fine."

"And the pilot?"

Henry shook his head. "I'm afraid he wasn't that lucky. He did a fantastic job of bringing in that plane, but they had a rough landing. He didn't have much of a chance."

Henry led her to a seat and sat down beside her. "They aren't allowing any visitors, yet."

"Yes, Cynthia told me."

"Why don't you go on over to the house and get some rest? Once he starts stirring, you'll probably have your hands full." Henry smiled. "It's good to see you again, Emily. You've really had Jeremy going around in circles for months now. I'll be glad to see the two of you married. Maybe he'll be able to concentrate on his work a little more."

She didn't know what to say. She didn't know where she stood with Jeremy, and at the moment their relationship wasn't nearly so important as his survival. He might not even want to see her, and that was all right, too.

In the meantime, she'd wait because she had to.

"This has really been a shock. I wasn't expecting him back here until the weekend. He said he was going to Little Rock to pick you up." Henry seemed to realize what he was saying. "My God. That's right. You were supposed to have been on that plane with him, Emily. What happened?"

She shook her head. "We quarreled. It all seems so unimportant now, Henry. I didn't know he intended for me to go with him. He just left."

Henry shook his head. "He's been under tremendous pressure these last few months—trying to rearrange his schedule so he'd have time off for the two of you to spend together. And this mess with Linda took a great deal out of him."

"I know."

"Michelle's doing very well, considering. We told her that Jeremy's plane was delayed and he wouldn't be here for a while. She was disappointed, but at least she doesn't know how bad it was. Maybe she won't ever have to know."

They sat there together, and Emily had to face the heartache of regret. Jeremy had borne the brunt of her moods and insecurities. She wondered if he would ever be able to forgive her.

Cynthia drove Emily out to Jeremy's house. There she was greeted by Peggy, the housekeeper, whom she remembered from her first visit, just as Michelle came running into the hallway.

"Emily!" she cried, throwing her arms around Emily's waist.

"Hello, darlin'."

"Daddy isn't home yet. I'm so glad you're here. We can surprise him when he gets home, can't we?"

"I'd like that," she said, walking toward the living room.

"Dinner's on the table, Ms. Hartman," Peggy said. "I'll see to your luggage if you'll make sure Michelle eats. She's been too excited to eat." They exchanged glances, and Emily knew how hard it had been for Peggy to remain calm for Michelle's sake.

"Just leave my bag. I can unpack it later."

"You can sleep with me, okay?" Michelle asked, bouncing on her toes when Emily pulled the chair out for her.

"Okay."

"Oh, Matilda's going to be so glad you're here. She talks about you all the time."

"She does?"

"Uh-huh. She keeps talking about you and Daddy getting married. Are you?"

"Well, I—uh—"

"Daddy says you are . . . one day. But he never says which day."

"I see."

"But when he gets here, you can make him pick which day so I'll know. I have the prettiest dress to wear, and Matilda has a new dress and—"

"*Matilda* has a new dress?"

"Yes, 'cause she can't go to a wedding in her jumpsuit. She'd look silly."

"She certainly would."

"So Peggy made her a dress, and it's very pretty. Do you wanna see it?"

"Why don't we eat first, okay?"

"Sure. Now that you're here, we've got lots of time to do things together, don't we?"

Emily bit her lip. "Yes, we do."

Hours later, Emily managed to get Michelle to sleep, and then she called the hospital. Henry was still there, waiting. When he came on the line, he sounded more encouraged.

"The doctor let me take a peek at him about an hour ago. They've got him all hooked up to machines, and he looks pretty battered, but they assure me his vital signs are good and that he's in satisfactory condition."

"Oh, Henry" was all she could say.

"I know, babe, I know. This has been a rough one. I thought I'd hang around to reassure him about everything, just in case he regains consciousness."

"I know, Henry. You love him."

There was an embarrassed silence. "Yeah, you got that right. So how's Michelle?"

"She's doing very well. Very excited about my being here."

"I'm glad you came. You're going to be just what Jeremy needs."

"I hope so, Henry. I've been such a fool."

"Hey, join the human race, babe. None of us has the ability to go through life all the time with the style and grace we'd prefer. Jeremy doesn't expect perfection."

"Thank God," she muttered, and they both laughed.

"Call me if anything changes, okay?" she asked.

"Yes. Now you get a good night's sleep. I have a feeling you're going to find yourself up here tomorrow holding hands with our man."

She hoped it would be that simple.

The next morning she went looking for Michelle after breakfast and found her in the study, watching television. Upon closer inspection, Emily realized she was watching a video of Jeremy's concert.

"Hi, Emily. You wanna come watch my daddy sing? Mama's on here, too."

Emily sank down next to Michelle and put her arm around her. "Do you watch this very much?"

"Uh-huh. I like to see them. I like to see Mama smiling. She's happy now. Just look."

Emily watched the interview once more, this time feeling much more objective than when she'd first witnessed it. Now she heard what was being said. Linda was laughingly explaining that she had flown in to see Jeremy's show in order to let him know that she was engaged. Linda explained to the reporter that she was marrying a man that Jeremy had introduced to her. The man had spent a considerable amount of time with Linda while she was at the rehabilitation center. It was obvious that Jeremy was pleased for both of them.

Then Linda explained that Jeremy had agreed to allow her to join them because she wanted a chance to share what she had experienced and the help that she had gained through the rehabilitation program.

Jeremy could have denied her the airtime, and no one would have blamed him. Instead he had understood her need to share what could be done for others with problems too great for a family to cope with.

With her new objectivity, Emily could see that Jeremy was proud of Linda and the strides she'd taken toward recovery, but there was no hint of anything more than friendship between them.

What a fool she'd been, reacting to the interview with such irrational jealousy. No wonder Jeremy had been so annoyed.

When the concert continued, she sat there watching Jeremy as he performed, his high energy on the stage radiating out to the crowd who loved him and didn't care who knew it. She knew the feeling. For the first time, Emily could understand how a person could go to a public performance and scream and yell her love and adulation.

After the last cheering died down from the finale, Jeremy walked back out on stage and sat down at the piano.

"The following song is not on my latest release. In fact, it's one I've only recently completed, so the band doesn't have the score yet. If you don't mind my accompanying myself—" he paused while the crowd went wild "—I'd like to share it with you."

The chords he began to play were soft—a rippling effect that created a sense of intimacy in the huge arena. The crowd became so quiet that it sounded as though each person had forgotten to breathe.

When he began to sing, Emily caught her breath. He was singing a song about Emily. As he sang, he described in verse what having her in his life had meant to him, what dreams he'd had since knowing her, loving her, and his hope that someday she would understand what she truly meant to him. And the song ended with, "I give my love to you ... with all my heart."

The melody soared with its own intensity, the words following the intricate line with ease. For a few moments after he played the last few chords, the audience was still, and then it went wild.

He stood up from the piano and waved. The camera came in for a close-up. Jeremy's face was lit up, obviously pleased with the reaction. Emily had never seen him look so excited.

Michelle slid off the sofa and trotted to the video recorder. "That's all of it. Wasn't that a good show, Emily?"

Emily fought for control as she realized the enormity of what she had done, and what she hadn't done. She had told Jeremy that she had seen the concert, and she hadn't mentioned the song.

No wonder he had felt she didn't love him. Who could blame him? He'd written her one of the most beautiful love songs she'd ever heard—the melody alone would haunt people for years to come—and had offered his love and his heart to her in front of millions of people.

And she hadn't said a word to him.

* * *

Two more days passed before the doctor agreed to allow Jeremy to have any visitors. When Henry told Jeremy that Emily was there, and that she had arrived only hours after the crash was reported, he asked to see her.

She didn't know how she was going to be able to handle the meeting, because she didn't know how he felt about her being there. Would he still be remembering their last words to each other? Would he be pleased she was there? Never had she faced anything with so many mixed emotions.

Henry pointed out Jeremy's room to her and said he was headed home for a few hours. Henry had stayed at the hospital around the clock until the doctor assured him that Jeremy's steady improvement was not based on the fact that Henry was there.

Pushing the door open, Emily entered the silent room. There were several flower arrangements sitting around, and Henry had told her that these were only a few that had been sent to Jeremy when news of the accident was broadcast. Every patient in the hospital had received at least one floral gift.

She paused at the end of the bed and looked at him. One side of Jeremy's face was bandaged, and the other side was swollen and discolored. His arm was in a cast, and his chest appeared to be heavily bandaged.

But he was alive. She could see the movement of his chest from where she stood. He lay with his face toward the window, and the subdued light showed him to have some color in addition to the bruising.

There were dark circles under his eyes, and she remembered what he'd said about returning to Las Vegas and sleeping for weeks. He was certainly going to find the time for that now.

She came around the bedside and picked up his hand, bringing it up to her mouth and placing a kiss on his palm.

His eyes opened, and he stared blankly at her a moment, then ran his tongue along his dry lips.

"Emily? Is it you?"

"Yes, Jeremy, I'm here," she said, her voice catching.

He closed his eyes for a moment. "Thought I was dreaming," he said after a pause.

"I finally got to hear the song you wrote for me. I missed it the first time I saw your concert."

His eyes searched hers as though trying to read a message in them, but he didn't say anything.

"It was so beautiful, Jeremy. You have such a wonderful way of expressing yourself, both in words and music."

"I thought you were angry," he finally said, his voice a mere whisper.

"About what?"

"The song. That I expressed my feelings so publicly. I thought that was the real reason you were angry."

"Oh, Jeremy, no. I had no idea when you were there that you'd written the song or performed it. I feel very honored."

His mouth twitched into a half smile at her words. "I live my life on a stage," he managed to say. "You're right about that."

"I don't care. To be loved by Jeremy Jones is something to shout about."

He closed his eyes, as though her words had pained him. She stood there, not knowing what to do. She continued to hold his hand, loving the feel of him.

"You haven't been doing any shouting," he said finally.

"The nurse would throw me out of here, or I would be shouting, don't kid yourself."

He opened his eyes, and this time they seemed brighter. "You mean that?"

"I love you, Jeremy. I've loved you ever since I met you, and I couldn't have hidden it if I tried."

"Could've fooled me," he whispered.

"If you haven't given up on me, I want so much to marry you. And I'll be happy to go on the six o'clock news tonight and announce the fact."

His eyes grew brighter. "I'd enjoy seeing that."

She leaned over and kissed him. "Then you're going to have to hurry up and get out of here."

He was quiet, but she was no longer worried about his silence, because his eyes were so eloquent. Finally he said, "Henry said Michelle's keeping you entertained."

"She certainly is. She and Matilda already have their dresses to wear for the wedding."

He smiled, a smile so tender she thought her heart would melt.

"I'm glad somebody had faith."

"So am I, love. So am I. The trouble with me is that I didn't really believe that fairy tales come true."

"But now you do?"

"Oh, yes. As soon as you've recovered, I intend to plan the splashiest wedding that Michelle could ever imagine, so that we can start on our happy-ever-after."

His hand slowly tightened on hers, then relaxed. "I love you, Emily. So much."

She could see that he was tiring, and she knew she would have to leave him, at least for a little while. But once he was released, she knew she'd never leave him again.

"I love you, too, Jeremy. With all my heart."

Epilogue

Jeremy and Emily slipped into their seats only minutes before the opening ceremonies of the Academy Awards. She glanced at Jeremy from the corner of her eye and bit her lip to hide her smile.

In the ten years they had been married, she had never seen him so nervous. But then, this was the first time he'd ever been nominated for an Academy Award for one of his musical scores.

She reached over and took his hand. He gripped hers and smiled at her.

"Have I told you how ravishing you look tonight, Mrs. Jones?" he drawled.

"You might have mentioned it a time or two, yes," she admitted with a grin, "but I never get tired of hearing it."

After ten years Emily was used to being on display, used to flashbulbs popping in her face, used to seeing her picture alongside Jeremy for whatever reason.

"What a mob scene," he muttered, looking around.

"You know you love it," she said.

"The trouble with you is that you know me so well," he admitted. He looked over his shoulder. "What happened to Michelle?"

"She wanted to check her makeup and make sure her hair was in place before she sat down next to you. After all, the cameras will be flashing all evening."

"So why aren't you nervous?"

"I'm used to it. Besides, with you around, nobody ever notices me."

"Hah," he said, leaning over and kissing her just below the ear.

He knew what that did to her, knew every place on her body that came to a quivering life of its own whenever he touched her. And he took full advantage of the information whenever possible.

"Dad! You're worse than a teenager necking in the theater," Emily heard Michelle say. Glancing past Jeremy, she saw her stepdaughter sit down on the other side of her father. "You could at least wait until they dimmed the lights," she hissed in a low voice.

Jeremy laughed and hugged Michelle. "What would I do without you keeping me in line?"

Emily thought Michelle looked beautiful tonight and much older than her fifteen years. She wore a blue satin dress that set off her light brown hair and dark eyes. The style was simple yet very elegant. She had the figure to wear it well.

Settling back into her seat, Emily placed her hand on Jeremy's thigh and gently stroked him.

He leaned over and whispered, "None of that, woman, or I'll end up embarrassing both of us, dimmed lights or not."

She placed her hand demurely in the crook of his arm and gave him an innocent smile. "Just trying to distract you, dear."

"You're doing a hell of a good job."

Life with Jeremy Jones had never been dull. From the time they'd announced their engagement, within days after his release from the hospital all those years ago, right up to this evening's events, Jeremy Jones's every move seemed to be news.

Emily had long since learned to take it in stride. Of course Jeremy had helped her adjust, shielding her from the more aggressive reporters, stepping in and assisting whenever the questions seemed to be unnerving her. He'd even taught her to prepare answers to questions that she didn't want to answer, because sooner or later they would come up.

He'd won the battle with Henry about tours. Tours became associated with the plane crash for Henry, and he decided that Jeremy could find other ways to promote his music.

In the meantime, Jeremy bought several acres of countryside near Hot Springs in Arkansas, and built a beautiful multilevel home. They spent most of the year there. He worked hard writing music, and Emily managed to keep herself busy.

He still performed in Las Vegas twice a year, but he had sold his home there. They leased a place during the weeks they were in town.

"Mom?"

From the impatient sound of her voice, Emily realized that Michelle must have called her more than once.

"Yes, darling?"

"Did you really tell Andy he could stay up tonight and watch the awards?"

"What did he tell you?"

"He said that he and Carmen were going to stay up and eat popcorn with Ryan and watch television."

"That's true. Ryan was going to let them watch in his room."

"Andy'll never stay awake that long. He's only three years old."

Jeremy interposed a comment. "Emily is aware of how old he is. She was pregnant during that horrible heat wave we had that year."

"I just don't understand why you're letting them all stay up, even if Dad may win."

"What do you mean *may*," Emily asked with a smile. "Of course your father is going to win. I saw no harm in allowing all of his children to watch."

Jeremy grinned. "Michelle, think about it for a moment. We're out here on Pacific time when the kids are used to Central. They're all used to going to bed at eight; that's eight o'clock *Central* time." He glanced at his watch. "I wouldn't be surprised if all three—even Ryan, though he's a grown-up nine years old—are asleep by now."

Michelle began to laugh. "What a dirty trick. You gave them permission, knowing full well they'd never be able to do it."

"Why not? It won't hurt them to sleep in Ryan's room until we get back."

Michelle glanced around the crowded room. As soon as her attention wandered away from them, Jeremy leaned over and said, "I didn't think she'd appreciate my pointing out that we used to do the same thing with her when she was Carmen's age."

"Probably not."

He sighed, linking his hand with hers. "It's hard to believe that all of this started ten years ago."

"I know. Michelle refused to believe that the way we met was because I won a contest to be your date for the evening."

"You have to admit that's rather bizarre."

"What's bizarre about it is that you fell in love with me. I'm sure Henry didn't have that part worked into the idea."

"Only because he didn't think of it. Otherwise he would have. Look at how he played up that angle when we got engaged."

"I was so afraid."

"Yes. I remember."

"And my fears were so foolish."

"I believe I've pointed that out a few dozen times, as well."

"You were right. Loving somebody means letting go of all those fears and trusting that love will help to smooth the way."

"I haven't heard you complaining that our love caused any bumps in our paths."

She touched his cheek. "No. You taught me what love is. I'll never forget it. I want our children to fully understand it, as well."

He glanced around at Michelle, whose sparkling eyes excitedly took in the scene. "If she's any indication, we're on the right track." He shifted in his chair. "I just hope she's not disappointed if I don't win tonight."

"Jeremy. We all know that you're a winner, whether or not you come home with a little statuette."

"Thank you for those kind words."

"And thank you—for all the love you've given me...given all of us. I never knew happy-ever-after could be so much fun."

He laughed. "Oh, happy-ever-after's just beginning, love. I promise—with all my heart."

*   *   *   *   *

ATTRACTIVE, SPACE SAVING BOOK RACK

Display your most prized novels on this handsome and sturdy book rack. The hand-rubbed walnut finish will blend into your library decor with quiet elegance, providing a practical organizer for your favorite hard-or soft-covered books.

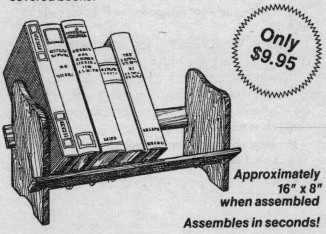

Only $9.95

Approximately 16" x 8" when assembled

Assembles in seconds!

To order, rush your name, address and zip code, along with a check or money order for $10.70* ($9.95 plus 75¢ postage and handling) payable to *Silhouette Books.*

Silhouette Books
Book Rack Offer
901 Fuhrmann Blvd.
P.O. Box 1396
Buffalo, NY 14269-1396

Offer not available in Canada.

BKR-2A

*New York and Iowa residents add appropriate sales tax.

 **Silhouette Desire**

COMING NEXT MONTH

#439 THE CASTLE KEEP—Jennifer Greene
Although architect Micheal Fitzgerald had made a career out of building walls, he'd never seen defenses like Carra O'Neill's—defenses he planned on breaking down with a little Irish magic.

#440 OUT OF THE COLD—Robin Elliott
When Joshua Quinn was sent to protect Kristin Duquesne, he wasn't supposed to fall in love with her. But he had . . . and now both their lives were in danger.

#441 RELUCTANT PARTNERS—Judith McWilliams
Elspeth Fielding had her own reasons for agreeing to live in a rustic cabin with James Murdoch. But after she met the reclusive novelist, the only important reason was him!

#442 HEAVEN SENT—Erica Spindler
A fulfilling career was Jessica Mann's idea of "having it all"—until she met Clay Jones and fulfillment took on a very different meaning.

#443 A FRIEND IN NEED—Cathie Linz
When Kyle O'Reilly—her unrequited college crush—returned unexpectedly, Victoria Winters panicked. She *refused* to succumb to her continuing attraction, but she could hardly kick him out—it was his apartment.

#444 REACH FOR THE MOON—Joyce Thies
The second of three *Tales of the Rising Moon*. Samantha Charles didn't accept charity, especially from the high and mighty Steven Armstrong, but a twist of fate had her accepting far more!

AVAILABLE NOW:

#433 WITH ALL MY HEART
Annette Broadrick

#434 HUSBAND FOR HIRE
Raye Morgan

#435 CROSSFIRE
Naomi Horton

#436 SAVANNAH LEE
Noreen Brownlie

#437 GOLDILOCKS AND THE BEHR
Lass Small

#438 USED-TO-BE LOVERS
Linda Lael Miller

Silhouette Intimate Moments

At Dodd Memorial Hospital, Love is the Best Medicine

When temperatures are rising and pulses are racing, Dodd Memorial Hospital is the place to be. Every doctor, nurse and patient is a heart specialist, and their favorite prescription is a little romance. This month, finish Lucy Hamilton's Dodd Memorial Hospital Trilogy with HEARTBEATS, IM #245.

Nurse Vanessa Rice thought police sergeant Clay Williams was the most annoying man she knew. Then he showed up at Dodd Memorial with a gunshot wound, and the least she could do was be friends with him—if he'd let her. But Clay was interested in something more, and Vanessa didn't want that kind of commitment. She had a career that was important to her, and there was no room in her life for any man. But Clay was determined to show her that they could have a future together—and that there are times when the patient knows best.
